Dakota and the American Dream

Sameer Garach

MARE PRESS

Cover Design by Canva
Stock Photo: Portrait of little boy in Uncle Sam costume walking with
        American flag, drawn by hand illustration | ID 134789971
        Copyright Victoria Plotnikova | Dreamstime.com
Author photograph by Sameer Garach
Dakota and the American Dream
Copyright 2019 by Sameer Garach
All rights reserved.
ISBN-10: 0-9990574-6-4
ISBN-13: 978-0-9990574-6-9
Library of Congress Control Number: 2019918858
Published in the United States of America by Mare Press, Houston, TX
MARE PRESS and MARE PRESS Design are trademarks of Mare Press.
Social media logos on the cover are trademarks of Facebook, Pinterest, and
        Instagram.

For America and its diverse and wonderful people.

The purpose of an American is to find his or her American Dream and go out and do it.

ACKNOWLEDGMENTS

Thank you for reading *Dakota and the American Dream*. It was a surprisingly short journey—less than a year—from the beginning of the first manuscript to publication of the last. My first book, *The Bull Option*, took three arduous years to compose; it was much longer—more than double this novel—and I was a novice writer. However, there were many bumps in the road to coming up with a workable story for *Dakota and the American Dream*; it wasn't until I looked for inspiration from Lewis Carroll's *Alice's Adventures in Wonderland* and examined the deeper meaning of what I was trying to write that I officially began my journey.

There are not a whole lot of people who contributed to this work; for one, I had next to nothing in my bank account when I wrote the novel, and two, I was more experienced at writing the second time around.

Nevertheless, I owe a debt of gratitude to Sonja Cassella and Desmond White, both of whom performed a beta read. They made a significant impact on my first book, so I tapped them again and fortunately they agreed.

At the Houston Writers Guild, I'd like to thank my talented Thursday morning critique group—Mark Andersen, Alicia Richardson, Lynn Long, and Tassie Kalas. They were instrumental in pointing out that much of my early draft was for adults and improving the satirical expression of the parody.

I reserve a special thanks to writer and creator Angela Thayer for giving me permission to make a derivative of her song, "A Color

Chorus." She runs a wonderful education blog at http://www.teachingmama.org, where she shares hands-on learning activities for young children.

I can't say thank you enough to Dr. Sarah Tyler for creating datayze, a website based on data and statistics. The Writing Assistance Apps helped me tremendously in writing to the appropriate grade level; as an adult with no children, it was fairly difficult to think and write like a child.

Last but not least, I'd like to thank my family. Without your continued support, I would not have been able to create a work of entertainment that is uniquely American.

I hope you enjoy *Dakota and the American Dream*. Thank you.

Chapter 1: Down Hopscotch Lane

Dakota was tired of playing catch with his mother at the park, and wanting to rest, he cuddled up to her on a bench, careful not to tip over the coffee cup she sipped at. He glanced at the laptop she was working on, once or twice. But it had no games to play or movies to watch, and Dakota thought, "What is the use of a computer if it has no games or movies?"

So he considered whether it would be worth the effort to mark out a good distance between two trees, sprint from one to the other, and time himself to see if a personal record could be set, when suddenly a fat squirrel with an olive green back hopped by him and gently chewed away at an acorn.

The rich olive green fur on the backside captured the attention of Dakota, who was very fascinated by it, so much that he hadn't even noticed the rodent's clothing—a dull gray suit jacket and an olive green tie—as he'd never seen such a coat before—only the gray and auburn variety appeared in his backyard. The curious hair made for a few blinks, but he was surprised to find that his eyes weren't playing tricks on him. "Perhaps," he thought, "I've eaten so many green apples, my eyes have warped!" (For, you see, Dakota's mother started an apple business some time ago that made apple pie, apple juice, apple chips, apple whatever, most of which Dakota had no taste for.) He brought his hands up slowly before his face, afraid he might witness a green hue, but there was no such thing, and he relaxed, except in another moment the Greenback Squirrel pulled out from its furry trouser pocket a

1

Fitbit—which had the time displayed—and said to itself in a most peculiar accent, "Whoa, I'm wicked late! Now, what'll be my fate?"

The spoken words summoned Dakota to edge closer and made him wonder how the Greenback Squirrel talked, but just as he did so, the rodent dropped his acorn and ran away, to the start of a game of hopscotch. The walkway had numbers and squares painted on it. Then he stopped and faced Dakota, as if he were inviting him to play, so Dakota started to his feet, for it occurred to him that the fat Squirrel was a curious calling, and overcome with desire, he hurried after the bushy tail down hopscotch lane and hopped from one box to another in pursuit of it, until he had gone up the trunk of an enormous tree—the lines continued up the tree—and the Squirrel vanished altogether down a hole.

In his haste, Dakota had failed to notice that he had gone up the side of the trunk as if it were perfectly normal to walk up trees. He turned around at once and, facing the painted lines on the trunk, backpedaled up the tree in fear and said to himself, "Holy seeds, I'm sure this is a dream!"

In another moment Dakota fell through the same hole, never once imagining such a thing could happen while playing hopscotch, and a look of fright marked his face as he dropped onto a curvy chute and started to slide. The dark space continued straight down like an elevator tunnel, but there was nothing he could grab hold of to stop himself, not even the ladder, which ran along the wall, as it was too far to reach. He huffed and puffed in agony, confused as to what was happening, and wondered how long he would slide.

First, he checked what he'd land on by peering over the edge but only saw darkness down below. A few objects—bottles of apple juice, jars of apple jam, and other apple products—stuck out the walls or rested on the steps of the ladder and glowed like light bulbs; they appeared and disappeared almost instantaneously. "Why are mom's apple things inside the tree? Oh, I know. This must be an apple tree!" little Dakota thought. As he gained speed, everything looked like a blur, and he could only catch a few items with his eyes.

The tunnel was deep because he slid fast and for a long time. And while he would have liked to enjoy the ride, for he fancied slides, it all happened so fast and unexpectedly, he couldn't get the normal thrill out of it. Having nothing to do but slide, Dakota regretted hurrying after the Greenback Squirrel and his desire to play the game. He could've done

2

just fine sitting where he was—in fact, he would've been delighted. But the rodent had challenged him to take part. So Dakota made up his mind right then and there that he would pursue this curious dream, rather than pinch himself awake, even if it were just an illusion, unless he found it disagreeable.

The chute curved sharply, burning Dakota's back, and he began to worry. "Will I ever stop sliding? This wouldn't have happened if Bernie was here. I'm sure he would have warned me." He started to miss his foot-high, furry friend. Bernie was a Saint Bernard puppy and had a big head, a short muzzle, dark eyes, and white-and-brown fur, all of which made him look gentle and friendly. Bernie was always there when Dakota had problems and would even rescue him if he could, like when a squirrel attacked Dakota in his backyard.

Then he thought about what Bernie would do with such a big hole, like the one Dakota found himself in. The dog might bury some bones or toys, though Dakota wasn't sure if the pup would ever return from the abyss. "What will Bernie do without me?" he said to himself. Bernie didn't have any friends except Dakota. "Who will play fetch with him now?" Dakota's mother sure wouldn't—she was busy with her apples—and his father couldn't—he worked downtown until late in the evening.

Dakota's ten-year-old mind skipped along, as he never could control his thoughts, and he suddenly wished he had Yellow Fellow, his fluffy, golden teddy bear, whom he slept with. (For, you see, though most children Dakota's age had outgrown the need for a plush toy, little Dakota was very attached to his; he was an only child, and Yellow Fellow made sure he was never lonely.) "I wonder if he misses me?" he thought aloud. "If I could only see his smiley face, I'd get through this." Yellow Fellow never stopped smiling, not even on sad days, and was always ready to offer a hug. "How did I forget to take him?"

Here the chute ended while he was worrying, and he flew out and screamed. There was a fast whoosh with a rustle, a flapping, and a most scary crunch. He yelled, thinking he'd broken a bone, but then realized he had landed on top of a pile of garbage bags. He was relieved that he wasn't dead or hurt but disappointed he wound up in garbage, endless garbage. Cardboard boxes, plastic bags and bottles, paper cups, uneaten food, and who knows what else enveloped him. A most terrible stench made him pinch his nose. And a few harassing flies caused him to wave his arm. "Shoo! Go away." Something crawled on his other arm and

3

warned him to *get the heck out*. He wormed himself out of the muck and tumbled down without so much as a scratch.

Once Dakota got to his feet and dusted himself off, he called after his parents, "Mom? Dad?" but no one was there. Everything had changed so fast, and he began to frown like never before. Dakota was all by himself in a New World, and no one could help. "Holy seeds, how will I manage? How will I go on?" he thought. His parents were always there when he needed them, but now he would have to do everything on his own.

A quick study of his surroundings revealed a red telephone booth, a few dingy lights on the walls, several chutes above him, and a wooden door at one end of a circular hall. He searched for a ladder; the one he'd seen along the wall had disappeared. If there were all these chutes, there ought to be ladders. Because chutes and ladders went together. But he found none and heard a scrunch from behind.

A few bags had dropped from a chute above, stunning Dakota, as they could have fallen on him. There was so much waste at the bottom of the park, he couldn't count the bags. It seemed as though the inhabitants of the New World were dumping their waste in nature. Dakota wondered who dropped the trash down the chutes. Did they know where the trash ended up? And why weren't they more responsible? If his teacher caught them polluting the world, they would've been in serious trouble.

Suddenly, the Greenback Squirrel sprang forth from the filth and said in his peculiar accent, fumbling the Fitbit, "Time is money, so now I must hurry!" He pocketed the little fitness band and scurried off toward the door. Away went Dakota like an arrow, and he gained on the bushy tail until it slipped through a doggy flap and disappeared, saying, "Out the cellar and to the cleansers!"

But lo and behold, a tiny peephole stared him in the face and squirted light on it, so he put his eye up to the hole and looked out at the tallest skyscraper there ever was. It was shaped like a standing octopus—wide at its ends, narrow in the middle, and shallow and domed at the top, with glass between the concrete arms—and surrounded by similar structures. Oh, how he longed to get out of the stinky room and ascend to the top of that building where he could gain a bird's-eye view of the city and touch the clouds, but the door, the door was a bit curious, for it was normal in every way, except the knob was high above his head, at the top of the door.

4

He knocked and waited, then banged on the door and waited some more, but no one answered. Poor Dakota stomped, burning with anger, for he'd never reach the handle. Everywhere he went, he had to be *this tall* or *that tall* to do anything; he couldn't ride roller coasters, drive a car, and drink the adults-only apple juice his dad drank once he returned home from work. All because he wasn't grown-up. "What a silly requirement!" he thought.

"And even if I was tall enough, it would be no use if the door was locked. I wish I was older, then I'd be taller. Oh, only if I could fast forward the process. When will I grow up?" But then it occurred to him that maybe he could stretch himself up. There were so many out-of-the-way things happening in the New World, perhaps anything was possible.

Dakota peeked inside the telephone booth, half hoping there would be a stool he could use to reach the doorknob, but nothing was in there except a phone. He picked it up and started dialing his home number, thinking he would soon talk with his parents, when suddenly water gushed out the earpiece. No sooner had his ear filled with water than he jumped out and found a pair of black dress shoes and a neatly-folded suit—a dull gray coat, matching pants, a white shirt, and a red clip-on tie—next to the booth. Maybe they were there all along, and he hadn't seen them earlier. It occurred to him that he had a shower, a curious one albeit, but a shower.

His first order of business: get rid of his dirty clothes and clean the muck off his body. So he peeked about, making sure no one would see him in his cartoon underwear, for that would be very embarrassing, and entered the booth and did what he set out to do, wondering all the while how he'd dry himself. When he finished, he pressed the numbers again, hoping the water would shut off. Not only did the water stop, the mouthpiece blew air like a dryer, and he dried. Dakota put on the new attire—it was a perfect fit—and started on his way, except there was the issue of the door.

He turned his head down and paced back and forth with some alarm, thinking of what to do, and just when he had given up, his eyes fell upon a work desk, which was not near the garbage before. He approached the table and found a small cough syrup bottle and a glass of water on it. "Holy seeds, where did this come from?" he asked in surprise and searched the room, but no one seemed to be present except

5

him. The bottle had a label on it which read, "TALLOXIN. Take once a lifetime. Reduces symptoms of shortness. Dr. Quack."

Now poor Dakota had a problem, and he knew medicine could fix problems. But could this syrup fix *his* problem? Some drugs made you drowsy and fall asleep. And Dakota had no interest in sleeping here. He'd taken medicine for coughs and colds before, but never anything for his height. He knew not to ingest any drug; the wisdom in him advised him not to take the mixture. Medicine had to be prescribed; otherwise, there might be side effects. "No, I'll see first who this is for," he said.

Wise little Dakota had enough intelligence to read and follow instructions because he'd seen what happened to children his age who didn't listen to the warnings that adults gave them. Like when some of them ran near the swimming pool and slipped and got hurt, or when they didn't wash their hands before eating and got sick, or when they wandered off at a public place and got lost.

But this bottle didn't say who the medicine was for, so he unscrewed the cap and smelled the contents—grape, his favorite—then waited a moment, thinking whether he should take the drug. If the label about reducing shortness meant what he thought it meant, then it should all be very fine. So he drank the syrup, then chugged down the water at once.

The grapey flavor of the syrup surprised him, as there was no hint of bitterness. But it was nothing compared to what happened next. "Holy seeds, I'm lengthening like a rubber band!" he said to himself. Within seconds, he started to grow, and his hands became larger, or the bottle became smaller. "How far will I stretch?" He began to worry because he'd seen a rubber band stretched too far. After a while rubber bands *broke*. "Oh, no, I might just snap."

"Bigger and bigger!" Dakota cried. Suddenly, the growth spurt stopped, it seemed. Now he was six feet high, and his face carried a brightness not seen since he'd come down here. He could reach the doorknob and go outside; it'd be a journey to get where he wanted to be, starting from the bottom, but he accepted the challenge. Whatever worries Dakota had of going on without parents disappeared, and he took courage as he viewed his hands and feet and felt his new power. "Wow! I'm a grown-up!" he said to himself. "I can take care of myself."

He spared no time to approach the door, for he might grow too tall, like a giraffe, and not fit in the doorway. And he wondered what it would be like to be so tall. He would be able to dunk a basketball very easily. Being tall was not such a bad thing. But he didn't want to be a giant, for then he might scare away his friends.

He turned the knob, and to his satisfaction, the door was unlocked.

Dakota and the American Dream

Chapter 2: An Interview with a Drone

Dakota opened the heavy wooden door and found himself in the park once again, except all the trees and plants were very big, and his new height made little difference. The rustling of leaves and the distant hoots of owls greeted him, and a dewy mist, which was common in the morning, came all around him. The door shut fast behind Dakota and echoed in the woods; he wheeled around and gaped, surprised to have come out of a large, fat tree whose door was flush with the trunk and lacked any sort of handle. He turned back around, half afraid of what he might find next, but a path lined with trees that went straight on like a hallway stood before him and led to the octopus-shaped skyscraper, so he began on his way.

As he marveled at the wilderness, he stumbled upon a tree which had a stairway going around it, and sparked with curiosity, he advanced up the steps, thinking he might get himself into a tree house, until he finally came to a branch which had a giant beehive hanging from it and another short branch that lowered to its doorway. "Holy seeds, I think it would be best to leave the bees alone," he said to himself. Dakota didn't dare to enter the beehive, for he had been stung by a bee before, right above his eye, and his whole eyelid had swollen and made it hard for him to see, and considering that everything was supersized in this park, the bees inside would likely be far worse.

So big Dakota began to withdraw his enthusiasm, except a female voice called out, "Go on! Don't be nervous"—down below, behind a tree, a spotted dog wagged its tail, and he imagined that it was the dog all along (for, you see, if the Squirrel could talk in the New World, maybe dogs could, too)—which gave him courage to believe it might turn out all right, and he went down the small branch.

Next, anxious Dakota poked his head in and peeked about, but seeing that there was no danger present, he entered, though still with a few doubts, and met a sticky floor, which required an extra bit of effort to lift his legs. An extraordinary smell of honey tickled his nose, as the space and counter were all made of honeycomb, which luckily had its holes filled with hardened honey so he wouldn't step into a hole and twist his ankle. Moreover, dull yellow paste covered the walls, dark stains marked the floor, and damaged hexagonal tiles spanned most of the ceiling, for some of the tiles had gone missing, and he could see the pipework above.

"Come in, we have an open door policy," a bee said in a raspy, feminine voice. She rose from behind the counter with glasses and makeup, and Dakota became puzzled, for he found it strange that a bee could be so friendly. Moreover, she had six legs—two for standing and four as arms—and wore a dull gray suit coat. "Sorry for the mess. The company sure picked a good time to move the hiring process out of the building. Human Resources is currently undergoing renovations."

"Hi, I'm Dakota," he said in a shy voice, unsure of what kind of conversation he should have with a bee.

"Glad you could make it. I'm Worker Bee. Your interview will start in just a moment. Please fill out the application in the meantime." She gestured toward a clipboard on the counter.

Dakota looked at the clipboard and leafed through several pages. Some of the questions on the papers were easy, like where it asked for your name and telephone number, but others made little sense, like where it wanted references and work experience. At the very end there was a line for his signature, and boy, did he want to show off his cursive John Hancock. He'd compare his autograph to others' in school and wow his classmates every time. Sometimes he'd write it down and stare at it for a while, amazed at how cool it looked. There was no doubt the Worker Bee would be impressed. "Excuse me," Dakota began politely, "what is this for?"

"We need an application," the Worker Bee answered. "I know it's a bore, but it's customary procedure."

The young man scratched his head, more confused than before, then peeked at the pages once more and said with a timid voice, "I— I'm not sure how to answer all of the questions."

"That's okay. Do the best you can." The Worker Bee returned to sorting papers on her desk. Dakota started to answer the questions with the responses a ten-year-old might give, and when he had gone through half of it, the Worker Bee interrupted him and said, "It's time for your interview. If you're not done, you can finish afterward."

So Dakota left the application on the counter and began to follow her down a hallway, where many colorful paintings hung on the wall.

Big eyes and an open mouth accompanied every painting he viewed. They looked nothing like the pictures he produced in art class—not an elephant, not a house, nothing. And the paint was thicker and had bumps and ridges when he touched it. Most of the paintings appeared to have occurred by accident, as though the painter had spilled the colors onto the canvas, or the artist had splashed a bunch of paints without care. Dakota was glad he could quit school after fourth grade and have a profession. "Why, I'll be an artist," he thought. The school library displayed his watercolors; maybe one day his work would hang in a beehive, too.

"Is there something wrong?" the Worker Bee asked, standing several feet ahead of him, near a doorway.

"Oh, no, I was just admiring the pictures," Dakota replied. His comment drew a confused and disappointed look from the Worker Bee, so he hurried to where she was standing and, inside a small space, found another bee sitting behind a hexagonal table, wearing a dull gray suit jacket.

"This is the Human Resources Drone, or HR Drone, your interviewer," the Worker Bee kindly introduced Dakota to the bee, then whispered into his ear, "It really is hard to get him to do anything, so if he quits his job, just tell me and I'll complete the interview."

"Dude, I like heard that," the HR Drone buzzed with a peculiar voice, which gave Dakota reason to believe the bee was not from around where Dakota lived. "I'm totally capable of conducting the interview."

"See to it that you do," the Worker Bee said in a contemptuous tone, then in a warm, pleasant voice to Dakota, "Good luck." She went back from where she came.

11

"Dude, can I like bum a pen off you?" the bee inside the room asked.

"Sorry, I don't have one," Dakota replied.

"Bummer! I'm like going to have to use this pencil," the Drone said. "Thanks for meeting us here for the job interview. Believe me, getting your foot in the door in Corporate America is like, not easy."

The last part was, of course, something Dakota could relate to, as he had great difficulty in reaching the high-positioned knob of the wooden door which led to the park. However, in another moment the type of interview he was about to have registered, and he couldn't help but say with a tone of shock, "Job? Holy seeds, but—but I'm so young!"

"Dude, don't sell yourself short. Anybody can like achieve the American Dream," the Drone said as a matter of fact. "Just give 110% in everything you do. You're already off to an awesome start, like thanks for dressing gnarly today. You can't imagine some of the applicants who have come in."

Dakota smiled, glad to have found business attire outside the telephone booth and a shower. He eased into the honeycomb-design guest chair in front of the Drone, as the compliment gave him reason to trust the talking bee.

"To start things off," the Drone said, "I'll tell you about the Creature Company—we really are a family here—and ask you some questions." The bee began talking about the company, or himself by starting his sentences with "we" or "our," which confused poor Dakota into a knot. Soon the boy lost interest and found it annoying that the bee kept speaking, especially with all the "likes" and "dudes," as though he were a teacher giving a lecture. At least Dakota's teacher let him participate in class. He thought about raising his hand once or twice, so that he could ask a question, but the Drone droned on—"we this" and "we that"—with no signs of stopping.

At first Dakota thought the Drone deserved a good swatting because it was quite rude to keep talking about oneself (for, you see, at school nobody liked braggarts). But on second thought, he made up his mind to stay where he was and not do anything, as slapping the Drone might not turn out to be such a good idea, for the bee would become alarmed and sting him.

Soon he politely raised his hand and waited to be called on. The Drone looked up at his hand and kept going, and going, and going, as if he were the Energizer Bunny from the commercials. And Dakota reasoned the bee might have eaten a good deal of honey with a lot of energy. He thought about blurting out something but checked himself to avoid interrupting the bee.

In another minute or two, the Drone concluded his boring speech and said, "That explains our mission, who we are, what we do. As you can see, we're a full-service business with a lot of moving parts. Now, my first question is: if you could be like any animal in the world, what animal would you be?"

Big Dakota smiled and thought, "What a silly question!" The question had come up not too long ago during lunch at school. At the time Dakota told his friends he wanted to be a lion. But lately he was thinking about being a dog like Bernie because it had rescued him from the squirrel in his backyard and was always very nice to him. And Dakota had never met a lion in person and wasn't sure he ever would, considering they were behind glass at the zoo.

"A dog," he answered, delighted to finally participate.

"Gnarly!" The Drone scribbled something on his clipboard, then asked, "Why don't woodpeckers, like, get headaches if they slam their heads on trees all day?"

Dakota thought before he spoke. He had read a book of children's riddles at the library and recalled stumbling upon this very question. "What a coincidence!" he thought. But he vaguely remembered the answer. His gaze turned up and to the right, as though there were an imaginary cloud with him viewing the riddles book there. The light bulb came on, and he answered at once. "They use their beaks, not their heads, so they get beak-aches."

"Dude, that's a hecka good answer." Again the Drone wrote something on his clipboard, and it seemed like he would continue doing so, so Dakota reasoned the bee was recording his responses, which made him feel as though he were taking an important test. Then the insect asked, "How does Santa, like, deliver presents to homes without chimneys?"

"Santa's not real," Dakota answered, very beat. Oh, he was tired of this question. It was such a hot-button topic at school for years and had been painstakingly decided that Santa was a myth. A riot nearly broke out in class when one of the children proposed that Santa was not in fact real. As the traditional belief of Santa's existence came under fire, questions naturally arose. "How can a fat guy visit so many houses in one night? With flying reindeer? It just is not possible," he thought. And some of Dakota's friends had witnessed their parents placing presents under the Christmas tree and gently eating the cookies and drinking the glass of milk set out for jolly, old Saint Nick.

While the Drone returned to his clipboard, with three questions in, Dakota was surprised to find an interview had so many childish questions. He thought grown-ups talked about grown-up things.

"Dude, you totally nailed the warm-up. Now, why do you like want to work here?"

"Oh . . . I'm not quite sure," Dakota said with a confused look on his face, then as kind as possible, "Sorry, I only went up the tree because I thought there was a tree house. But I really want to go to the city and see downtown."

"So, it's the *awesome* location that draws you? Well, the city does attract a grip of young people. There are like, *so* many things to do here," the Drone said, then repeatedly shook his head, as though he disagreed with Dakota. "But you could work anywhere and, like, still live in the city. So why do you want to work *here*?"

Dakota took another attempt by repeating his response, and curiously, the interviewer shook his head and asked the same question again, so Dakota responded with the same answer, thinking the bee had too much beeswax in his ears and was hard of hearing.

"Dude, please! Give us professional responses," the Drone ordered in a discouraging tone.

This, of course, did not set well at all with big Dakota, for the Drone kept hounding him, as though he were ready to sting. "I wish I could answer like an adult, but this new height is all too unfair. Oh, how strange it is to be a child stuck in an adult's body," Dakota thought. Then it occurred to him that if he took a page from some of the annoying children at school, the bee might be satisfied, so he mustered the most adult response he could. "I want to work here because it's the best place in the world."

As the Drone got what he was looking for, he stopped annoying Dakota and moved on to the next question. The bee only wanted to hear what he wanted to hear, like Dakota's teacher, and it occurred to Dakota that the children who kissed up in class were acting like adults.

"Most people in management are, like, hecka tall. Do you think size really matters?"

Upon hearing the question, Dakota's eyes widened with delight, and he answered, "Yes, because now that I'm taller, I can ride roller coasters and drive a car. I mean, I know how to drive bumper cars."

Dakota's response was met with laughter, and the Drone said, "Tubular response. I totally miss the days of bumper cars." Then he dropped the clipboard on the table at once and sighed. "Dude, this job is like, stressing me out," which gave Dakota reason to believe the interview was coming to an end, but the Drone went on, "What's the color of success?"

This was very easy for Dakota, and he chuckled as he replied, "Success is a word, silly. It has no color."

The Drone maintained a solemn face, then asked in a grave tone, "Dude, what are your weaknesses?"

"Everyone likes cookies, but I—" While it was true that many children Dakota's age had got their hands caught in the cookie jar, Dakota had a most troublesome habit of eating another sugary confection. "I love caramel apples and can't stop eating them!" (This was the one product his mother's apple business made that he liked.)

The bee stared at him for a moment or two, which gave Dakota reason to believe he had done something wrong, but then the Drone said at last, "An awesome sense of humor goes a long way. I totally love your honesty. Where do you see yourself in, like, five years?"

Dakota rubbed his chin, for the question had appeared on the application, but the poor child couldn't remember the answer he'd given, so he counted on his fingers to help and said, "Ninth grade."

"So, like, you want to gain some experience, then transfer to education?" the Drone reasoned—which only made Dakota turn quiet, as he was not sure what to say. "I'm stoked to hear that. Many people quit after a few years. What you learn here will like, be valuable wherever you go. It's awesome that you have a goal in mind. Some people come in here and, like, they don't know what they want to do. Well, that concludes the interview. Now, do you have any questions like about the work?"

There were only two concerns that came to Dakota's mind; the first was one of the only reasons he looked forward to going to school, so he asked, "Do we get recess?"

"A break?" The Drone yawned. "Dude, I could totally go for one now; I've never like worked so hard in my life. But to answer your question, sure, you can like take all the breaks you want, as long as you get the work done by the deadline."

"All the breaks I want, holy seeds!" Dakota exclaimed with a sparkle in his eyes, then pleased with the good news, he moved on to his next worry. "Will I have homework?"

"Sometimes, but dude, don't worry about it. Taking work home usually only occurs like during busy season."

And Dakota welled up with delight, for the necessary evil—homework—had been mostly done away with in Corporate America. He was beginning to see that there were more benefits that came with being an adult than just driving cars and riding roller coasters.

"When are you like, available to start work?" the Drone asked.

"Right now!" Dakota replied eagerly.

"I have a gnarly feeling about you," the Drone said, staring and nodding all the while.

Dakota wasn't sure whether an insect could have feelings, but anyway he was pleased to have started off on the right path.

"Now, let's see, should we hire you or not?" the Drone said with a sleepy voice. "The secret to getting hired is like, a lucky coin toss, so never get too down on yourself if it doesn't work out." Just then the Drone pulled out a coin from his jacket's pocket and positioned it ready for flipping. "Heads, you're hired, tails, you're not. Call it in the air."

"Heads," Dakota shouted as the Drone flipped the coin.

"Dude, no way!" the Drone said with a smile after catching the coin. "Welcome aboard! I'm stoked you got the job." He put out one of his hands, and Dakota shook it vigorously, feeling very proud that he passed the interview. Then he sat waiting for whatever would happen next.

"Dude, scram! I got to take a nap," the Drone said, so big Dakota walked out with his head held high and slowly made his way to the front, for he stuck around the hallway for an extra minute or two to view the artwork that he had only got a glimpse of earlier. When he returned to the honeycomb counter, the Worker Bee was nowhere to be found, and he exited just like he came—up the short branch and down the winding steps.

In another minute he went to scratch his head, for it was suddenly very itchy, but found his hair to be at his shoulders. This of course caused a great deal of worry, as it was a mystery how his hair had grown so much in such a short period of time.

At any rate the tall, octopus-shaped building stood a football field away, and he started on his journey. He played with his hair like the girls in his class, wondering what had happened to it, and at the end of the passage lined with trees, he came upon a stairwell that would put him on street level, so he headed for higher ground and found himself standing before the skyscraper.

Dakota and the American Dream

Chapter 3: The Pool of Money

Dakota had climbed the stairs to the entrance of the octopus-shaped skyscraper, or One Corporate Way—the address was engraved on one of the concrete arms—but scarcely had taken a few steps inside when an American Buffalo on its hind legs with a police badge and uniform suddenly yelled, "Stop, right there!" which startled Dakota to a halt. "Where do you think you're going?"

"Well—" Dakota swallowed as the Buffalo came out from behind a counter and stood over him. "I was just on my way to the top and—"

"Doesn't matter," the Buffalo cut him off, which Dakota thought was very rude, for he hadn't had the opportunity to explain himself. "You absolutely must wear a mask in Corporate America."

"But—but I haven't one," poor Dakota said in a trembling voice. "It's not Halloween, is it?" he thought. With so many out-of-the-way things happening, he wouldn't be surprised if it were. He began to worry that summer had gone by too fast, and the most curious part was that he hadn't remembered any of it, as if the season had disappeared from his memory. And he began to wonder whether summer even existed in Corporate America, for he had a fairly good memory, yet there was no recollection of playing with his friends or puppy, reading books, going on a family vacation, nothing.

"Come on, move it! Rules are rules," the Buffalo roared and started shoving him.

Big Dakota whined, "Why, I've never seen such rudeness, never!" Then with one big ram, the bison sent him right out the doorway. Poor

Dakota struggled to keep his balance and fell forward and tumbled down the stairs.

"Ouch! That hurt!" Dakota cried, then started to rub his arms and legs, and wherever he felt sore. "How am I in pain? A big boy like you should not be hurt no matter what. Or else, you'll be called a big baby! Come, there's no use in crying!" he scolded himself. (Big Dakota was very hard on himself, for, you see, he had high expectations for his grown-up self.) Nevertheless, he went on aching and crying. "Why does everything hurt so much?"

As he looked around him, his eyes fell upon coins on the steps that trailed to his pockets. "Why, I think that explains my feeling sore. I had a bunch of hard coins in my pockets." He stood with some trouble and began to empty his pockets—all the while wondering, "Whenever did my pockets fill with coins?"—until there was a pool of money all around him, about one foot deep, reaching down the streets. Surprised by the absurd amount of money, Dakota couldn't help but exclaim, "Why, I must have deep pockets!"

Soon Dakota heard a little tapping of shoes on the pavement and turned his head in the direction from which the curious noise came. Suddenly, the fat Greenback Squirrel appeared carrying a long bag around his shoulder and a white towel in one of his hands. As he raced past Dakota, he muttered to himself in his peculiar accent, "Oh, where has the time gone? The deadline is approaching wicked fast, and the Bigwig won't like that I'm late."

It occurred to Dakota that if the rodent was heading toward the building, he could ask him where he could find a mask, so as to enter One Corporate Way and get to the top, never once considering the great hurry the animal was in. Having no time to spare, for the Squirrel could be gone any second now, he yelled, "Excuse me—" with his arm out as though he were his dad calling for a taxi. But the Greenback Squirrel only jumped and dropped his towel, and nearly his bag before shifting it over his shoulder, very frightened, then hurried into the building as hard as he could go.

Dakota picked up the towel for two chief reasons: one, curiosity's sake; and two, it was very hot outside and he had worked himself into a sweat. And wearing a suit only made matters worse. He patted himself with the towel, then fanned himself with it in an attempt to create a small breeze, and switched back and forth between the two methods of cooling all the while wondering aloud, "Holy seeds, everyone is in a hurry here, yet it was only yesterday that things went at their normal pace. And oh, how I don't like the feeling of being rushed at all. The day seems shorter, for the summer has gone by and we're at Halloween! And my, oh my, I've changed so fast. Just yesterday I was small, and today I'm big!"

Next, he began to worry how he looked and said in a melancholy tone, "Maybe that is why the Greenback Squirrel became frightened and ran away. I'm sure it didn't like the way I looked—being this strange and tall, long-haired and all, is not good. I must be a scarecrow, for I am a terrible sight, indeed. They are made of straws, and I well, I look like a straw. I'm certain that is why the Buffalo wanted me to have a mask. Am I really that ugly?"

Then he started to think of a nursery rhyme to comfort him (for, you see, such songs had a soothing effect on Dakota). "Now that I'm not little I must sing something that is fit for my height. Because big people sing big people music and children sing songs for children. 'What are Big Boys made of?' That's what I'll sing." So Dakota cleared his throat and stood tall with his hand on his stomach, just as he would during music lessons, and listened to it rise and fall as he breathed. In another moment he began to sing from his stomach.

"What are big boys made of?
What are big boys made of?
Wholes and whales
And adult-giraffe tails,
That's what big boys are made of."

"Holy seeds, I'm afraid that doesn't sound the way it should," poor Dakota said in a sorrowful tone. "The lyrics came out all wrong anyway I feel worse than before. But come, there's some good in it: now I know you can't turn children's songs into adult ones. Indeed, it just does not work. Well then, I should think an adult song will help me manage better now that I'm an adult." So he sat on a step in the position in which you usually see *The Thinker* and thought for some time. After a minute or two, poor Dakota attempted another song, "Born in the USA" by Bruce Springsteen.

"Born down in a hospital room
The first kick I took was when I was in the womb

End up like a puppy that's been rubbed too much
'Til you spend half your childhood drinking from a sippy cup."

"I'm sure that is not the song that dad sings." So he tried to invent something; only it proved to be a failure. "Applesauce! I don't know any adult songs, or I have forgotten all of them, and now I shall go on feeling sad." ("Applesauce" was what his mother said to mean "nonsense.") He dug into his pockets and pulled out more coins, then said in a piteous tone, "Why, I have all this money and can buy all the ice cream in the world. I should feel good, right?"

As poor Dakota hung his head in defeat, he found his shoes to be a size too big for him; his ankles no longer pressed up against the back wall of the shoe, and he could wiggle his toes quite comfortably. He settled on a plan of action to tie his shoes tighter, but when he went down to do just that, his eyes fell upon his fingers, and he became alarmed. The fingers were skinnier than before—nothing more than bones with a thin coating of skin. The next course of action was to see his arm, so he pulled back one sleeve and saw that his arm had become as narrow as a pencil. This caused a great deal of worry, for he had never seen such a thing.

"Holy seeds, how could that have happened? I can't be getting any skinnier. Why, I'll just vanish altogether!" he said in a sorrowful tone. Last, he went to touch his face, half hoping it would be all right, but his chubby cheeks had disappeared. He stood and made an attempt to go over to the window to see his reflection, but his knees and hips wobbled, and he felt very strange, as though he were one of those circus people walking on stilts, and suddenly, he sunk into a deep melancholy.

In another minute he found that the cause of his strange nature had to do with all his sweating, for the towel in his hand was completely soaked, so he dropped it at once. "Why, I've lost all my water weight!"

"I think there should be outdoor air-conditioning. It would be of good use, indeed," Dakota said to himself, then in another moment, "Applesauce! I'm afraid after some time you would find it very cold—in any case jackets and sweaters every day."

Poor Dakota was getting tired under the hot sun, so he made up his mind to enter the building—for it would offer him shade—despite not having a mask. He began taking long, shaky strides up the steps and held the side rail to keep himself from falling over. "I'll tell the Buffalo

I'm about to go out because of dehy—" But he couldn't remember the word when you ran out of water and felt thirsty. "Dehy-water, or something of that sort, and the Buffalo will take good care of me because he's an officer."

He wiped the sweat off his brow with the back of his hand, the hand he used to hold the rail, then suddenly began to tip over and slipped on a coin. In another moment he flipped up in the air, and his landing made for a great splash in front of the building. Money was up to his chin. At first poor Dakota thought he had fallen into a bank's vault (for, you see, that was where the bank kept all the valuables). However, it soon occurred to big, wobbly Dakota that he had fallen into the pool of money which he had taken out of his deep pockets.

"More money, more problems!" Dakota said, as he moved about the coins. "Holy seeds, how curious today is. Come, there is no use in having all this money. I should think it is rather meaningless. Why, there is no shortage of money in this New World."

The next minute the sun went behind the clouds, and it seemed that it would stay like that for some time, as the weather began to look rainy, and a curious splashing came from some distance away in the pool. He quickly swam over (this was a dream after all) to see what was happening. At first he thought it might be another person, or maybe a cat or dog, but then out popped the head of a Black Rat.

Dakota and the rodent stared at one another for a moment or two without saying anything. The little rat wiggled its little nose; then tears of despair streamed down its solemn face. Dakota had never met a rat before, certainly not face-to-face, nor seen one cry. "Holy seeds, are you okay?" he started, then checked himself, for he found it rather strange to be talking to a rat. But when he gave it some thought, he reasoned that the rat might be like the Squirrel and Drone. So he tried again, "Oh, Rat, why are you sad? Oh, rat-a-tat-tat, Oh, rat-a-tat-tat. I smell a rat." Dakota smiled at himself and thought this might be a song, and if it wasn't, it could certainly be one. The rodent glanced at him, puzzled, then looked away.

"I think if I show the Rat that I'm harmless and want to be friends, he will help me find a mask," Dakota thought. So Dakota looked all around him and found a nice orange marigold that had been uprooted from a bed of flowers a small way off during the flood. (He knew what kind of plant it was, for, you see, he had planted the flower in his backyard with his mother before.) He brought the flower to the Black Rat, half hoping the rodent would accept it and not turn away.

"Chill out, bro! Why you come at me like that?" the Black Rat said at once in a peculiar accent and wiggled his nose. "First, my crib get flooded, and now you wanna stink me out? What the matter with you?"

To Dakota's delight the rodent could talk, albeit an unfamiliar variation of normal English. After his initial surprise went down, he addressed the Black Rat, "Oh, I'm sorry. I quite forgot that you do not like marigolds."

"Not like marigold? They be annoying. Nasty, stinky things," the Black Rat said in a shrill and passionate voice. "Would you stick your nose up in one if *you* were me?"

"Well, if I was a rat, I think I would not," Dakota said rather wisely, for he remembered one of the reasons why he and his mother had planted marigolds, peppermint, and other herbs in their backyard—to keep the rats out. "Oh, please don't be angry. I was only trying to be friends."

"Nah, I'm cool, ain't nobody tripping here," the Rat went on with his strange language. "But for real though, if you wanna be homies, then help me find my squad—my bae and her sistas, my bros—and my auntie. This flood done destroyed my crib."

"Oh, it was an accident," Dakota pleaded. It never occurred to big, wobbly Dakota that his money would create so many problems, not just for himself, but others, too. He quickly swam around the pool of money he made in pursuit of the Black Rat's family. He wished Bernie were present, for the dog could pick up the rat's scent and swim to the bottom of the pool and bring back his family. Bernie was such a resourceful and helpful dog. After a minute or two, Dakota's search turned out nothing, so he returned to the rodent.

"If only my dog Bernie was here, he would find your family. I'm sure of it," Dakota said as a matter of fact.

"Dog? Yeah, like a mutt gonna help. All they does is bark and chase us," the Black Rat stated in an offended tone. "Stupid *haters*."

"*Gators*? Well, maybe, but Bernie is such a nice puppy. He's very helpful and has a very good nose, and he could smell you and follow your scent and find your family and bring them back in his mouth." Just then the Black Rat rolled up the sleeves of his pajamas and started splashing coins at big, wobbly Dakota. "Oh, I'm sorry. I didn't mean to say that. Bernie isn't like other dogs. If you got to know him, I'm sure you would like him." The Black Rat turned his head away and started to swim in the direction from which he came. So Dakota settled on a plan of action to not mention his dog anymore, as the rodent was rather sensitive. "But let's not talk about the subject anymore. Oh, don't be mad at me. I'm good to rats; in fact, I know a rat, my friend's."

The rodent turned around and said, "Oh, word?" which only puzzled big, wobbly Dakota, who was getting quite tired of trying to understand the Black Rat. In another moment the rodent returned to Dakota and said, rather sharply, "And what does your homie plan to do with this rat, chunk it to a dog?"

"Oh, no, he's a Fancy Rat," Dakota began, glad to start a new conversation, then in a solemn tone, "but I'm afraid he doesn't talk quite like you do."

"Of course not. He a Fancy Rat," the Black Rat mocked. "He too bad to hang out with basic rats—like me. He wanna rub shoulders with the human crowd. I don't care."

"Yes, well, he's a very nice pet rat that lives in a cage, and—"

"A cage!" the Black Rat screamed.

"Yes, it's a very nice cage, made of metal. And it has three stories and a hammock for the rat to relax. Oh, I am jealous indeed; I wish I had a hammock. And his house—oh, he has a hut, which has a round doorway. Can you imagine that? There's a wheel, too, the rat's own personal gym, so it can exercise, and—"

"But it still be a cage," the Black Rat said in an offended tone. Then he pointed at Dakota and went on, quite sharply, "You one messed-up cat—a colorist, ain't you? Don't matter how hard we work; we can't never escape colorism. And I thought we done made it past slavery. When y'all gonna learn?"

"Oh, dear Rat, I'm not sure why I should apologize, but I'm not a colorist," poor Dakota argued, though he was quite uncertain what a colorist was. "I'm not sure why you're so offended. It's just so that the Fancy Rat doesn't get loose and go around the house."

"We ain't never cause no trouble, son," the Black Rat said in an angry tone and picked up some coins before adding, "Boy, if you don't hush your mouth . . ."

Luckily for Dakota, the rodent didn't hurl the coins at him as before. "I should be more careful talking to him," he thought. He began to twirl his locks, which had grown to his belly button now, and tried to think of all the things that might offend a rat, then said, very politely,

"We won't talk about flowers, or cages, or dogs. Please, dear Rat, don't be mad. I just want to be friends."

"You best not talk about them things. Who you think you is, come up walking in here like you owned the place? You lucky I ain't chunk this chump change at you," the Black Rat said in a severe tone. And in a minute or two he calmed himself down to a silence, for he stopped breathing so hard and put down the coins. "Let's go over to them steps. I'm gonna tell you about my struggle, and you gonna see why I ain't dig flowers and all them things."

And it was a good time to get out of the money for several other creatures—all wearing pajamas—were surfacing. There was a Green Lizard and a Blue Frog, then a Brown Ferret and a White Mouse, and some of them came in multiples, twos, threes, and up to sixes. The Black Rat led the way, and Dakota and the animals gathered on the steps of the building.

Chapter 4: A Rat Race and a Work Experience

They were very much a dirty bunch that had assembled on the walkway between the steps and the building—the rodents with their muddied fur, the amphibians with their slimy skin, and the reptiles with their dry scales, all smelling foul, covered in sewage, and upset.

When the Black Rat started to tell his struggle, the others quickly talked over him and voiced concerns about their future. The most important issue was of course settling who would inherit the wealth and reign and lead the sewer society (for, you see, Dakota kept the fact that he had ruined their homes with his money to himself). They had a small meeting about this matter for some time, and once they came to a resolution, Dakota found himself talking with them as though they were all close friends. He even had a heart-to-heart chat with the Brown Ferret, who at one point invited Dakota to visit his home once the streets cleared, to which Dakota gladly accepted, though he was quite uncertain how he would ever manage to visit a creature in the sewer, not to mention whether he wanted to. They became so close that an argument sprang up without any of them feeling offended, like old chums, and it was settled when the Ferret claimed in a rather snobbish tone, "I have more wealth than you, and therefore, I'm more important," then stuck his tongue out. Now Dakota refused to accept this argument, as he did have a great deal of money in his piggy bank, and pressed the Ferret to show his reserves, but when the creature failed to produce his bank balance, nothing more was said.

At last the Black Rat, who seemed to be a formidable leader due to his large size, stood on his hind legs in front like a teacher in a classroom and started in a proud and arrogant tone: "Listen up, listen up, everyone, I know how to settle the matter of who should lead our society. Hear me out, I got this." They all slowly turned to face him, as though they were reluctant to hear what he had to say, while Dakota swept his long hair to the side and kept his eyes fixed on the rodent, for he was eager to learn how the creatures would manage all his money and how their society functioned.

"All right, check this out," the Black Rat said with a loose air about him, punching his palm with a fist, then holding his hand, "Y'all ready for this? The Blame Game. We play the Blame Game." A few of the animals voiced *meh*s and their shoulders drooped; in general, there was little enthusiasm. However, the Black Rat went on, "We take turns blaming one another for this crazy disaster. Whoever be blamed the least be the winner and should get all the money and lead our society. With that being said—"

"Ugh," the White Mouse said in a tone of disgust with a shake of his little head.

"What the problem is?" the Black Rat asked rather sharply, then stared down the White Mouse so severely that he seemed ready to quarrel. "If you got something better, I'd like to hear it."

The White Mouse only sighed and rolled his eyes, then said with a flat voice, "No, go ahead."

"So, like I was saying, before I was interrupted," the Black Rat went on, rolling his eyes, which big, wobbly Dakota thought was very rude, "I blame the White Mouse for all our problems. The White Mouse—"

"Oh, please, for the love of God"—the White Mouse threw his hands in the air—"how on earth is this my fault?"

"The White Mouse was created a devil, to bring chaos upon this sewer. You"—the Black Rat pointed angrily at the White Mouse—"your ancestors—"

"Oh, yes, let's all point our claws to the easy and familiar target, the White Mouse," the rodent said with an air of disappointment. "You're living in the past, Black Rat."

In another moment the Black Rat's head jerked back, and his eyes widened, very shocked, and he said in a sulky tone, "Who you calling

Black Rat? Why can't you just call me Rat?" The rodent looked over to the others for support. "Y'all see the game being played?"

"No, I don't know what game you're referring to," the Ferret said rather sharply. "Why don't you explain it to us?"

"I know what you mean," the Lizard chimed in in an encouraging tone.

"Your fur is black, you sewer rat!" the White Mouse argued.

The Black Rat glared at the White Mouse and breathed heavily, and Dakota thought the whole matter to be absurd.

"Carry on, carry on." The Blue Frog yawned. "And by the way, I blame the Bush Rat. He *was* the leader. So, it must be his fault—" He ribbitted twice, then went on. "Why, excuse me. That grasshopper I had for breakfast is giving me quite the gas."

Then the Green Lizard added, "Poor fellow, that Bush Rat. Came from such a good family. He still hasn't shown up. I wonder what has become of him."

While the creatures turned their heads down in despair, the Black Rat withdrew from charging at the White Mouse and moved his eyes to big, wobbly Dakota. "Who you blame?"

"This game is taking us nowhere," Dakota replied in a melancholy tone. "We need a solution, not more finger pointing!"

"Exactly what I was thinking." The White Mouse nodded at Dakota with conviction in his eyes, then added, "I believe I have a better idea." He circled around to the front of the group and began with an air of bravado. "I say we end this outrageous, absurd, and most terrible Blame Game and start afresh. What say all of you?"

Cheers and claps immediately followed from the group, but the Black Rat's face turned down and gloomy, and he appeared to shrink away from the focus of attention, behind the White Mouse in his shadow.

The White Mouse went on, very firm in tone, "I motion for an entirely new and different match that will solve our problems, one that will revive our spirit, end our bickering, and provide lasting peace in our society. The best thing to restore order I propose is to have a Mouse Race."

The animals nodded, and tears of belief and meaning began to well in their eyes.

Meanwhile, Dakota twirled his locks, confused as to what a Mouse Race was.

The Black Rat stepped forward. "Why you got to name it after you, huh? Why can't you say, 'Let's have a Rat Race'?" He turned to the crowd and said, "Y'all dig what I'm saying?"

Everyone remained quiet and still. The smiles turned into frowns, and some of the creatures tsked and crossed their arms.

"Fine, we'll call it a Rat Race, happy?" The White Mouse looked at the Black Rat from the corner of his eyes, and his teeth chattered, annoyed. "It's the White Mouse's Burden to provide civilization to you, black pest," he muttered in a tone of contempt, which Dakota thought was very rude and would be certain to start a fight, but the dark rodent only frowned and remained speechless. The White Mouse addressed the crowd once again in an unfazed tone. "This Rat Race shall be the new way of life, a fair and equal way in which we can settle who deserves the wealth and power. The rightful owner shall prevail."

The crowd cheered and nodded again, without so much as to question the speaker. Meanwhile, the Black Rat found his way back into the crowd and became invisible.

Dakota raised his hand to inquire about the Rat Race, but quickly put it down because, from the looks on the animals' faces, everyone seemed to understand what a Rat Race was, or they just liked what the White Mouse had said, which Dakota had to admit did sound very good, and he didn't venture to stand apart from the crowd, for he didn't want to look stupid by asking a question everyone knew the answer to. But then he remembered his teacher saying that there were no stupid questions, only stupid answers. So with a timid voice, big, wobbly Dakota asked, "What *is* a Rat Race?"

"It is a competitive struggle to determine who is the wealthiest and most powerful. And the best way to learn is to participate," the White Mouse said in a welcoming tone. Then the rodent faced the group and, using his hands to signal the way, announced, "Animals of the sewer, make a loop around three blocks and return here at once." The creatures lined up facing different directions—some appeared to be ready to side-step the race, while others would move backward, and a few faced forward like they should. Then the White Mouse pointed to the dark rodent, who seemed all but forgotten, and said, "You there, Black Rat, you must have a delayed start. Stand back."

Of course the Black Rat protested that the White Mouse was a colorist, but the White Mouse would hear nothing of it, and the others did little to fight the unfairness the Black Rat met. "It is in the rules," the Mouse argued, "and the rules cannot be changed. If you cannot abide by our ways, then you shall not be a part of our society."

So the Black Rat stepped back and started several feet behind the others.

"On the pop, begin." The White Mouse retrieved a little firecracker and matchbox from the bed of flowers that had been uprooted—they seemed to have been hidden there for situations such as this—lit the fuse, then hurried off before the noise maker exploded.

The others waited for the bang, and when it did not come, as the firecracker was a dud, they ran with all speed in the direction of their choice, leaving Dakota to repeatedly ask, "Where is the pop?" as he was accustomed to following rules back home.

As Dakota watched the creatures run on the space between the steps and the building and swim in the streets, some turned the corner after one or two blocks, while others hid behind a corner for a short time and came back the same way. One by one, the animals gathered at the spot they started and panted, some more than others, with their hands on their knees, as the ones who breathed heavily had run a longer distance. The Black Rat returned first, and the White Mouse paced and looked around anxiously, then picked up a coin and announced the rat's victory.

"On behalf of the sewer, I'd like to present to you an award for your achievement," the White Mouse boasted as though he had won the coin himself, and the Black Rat accepted the token of approval and started dancing at once while the others watched. Once the celebration was over, the White Mouse whispered, "See, I *gave* you the victory. I am not a colorist as you claim."

"Gave? No, no, no," the Black Rat said in a sulky tone all the while shaking his head and wagging one of his claws. "I see you throwing shade at me, but I bust my hump and earned this victory."

"Yeah, because you cheated," the Frog snorted.

An uproar sounded from the sewer creatures, each protesting that the Black Rat cheated and each with a different reason as to how he did so. The Ferret said he cut corners and was lazy. The Frog argued that the Rat's handicap of starting behind everyone was a head start. The White Mouse claimed that the Rat used black magic and cast evil spells on all the other creatures, and this gave him black privilege. Furthermore, the Mouse went off about his advantages, like getting to label others as colorists. To which the Black Rat argued that it was nothing more than a figment of the white imagination. Despite the complaints, the Black Rat refused to back down and give up his victory; he argued that he was chosen and that everyone was a jealous *gator*, which made no sense to Dakota whatsoever, as there were no alligators in sight.

At last Dakota became impatient with the absurdity of the matter and said, rather severely, "You all cheated. I caught all of you red-handed!"

The animals looked at their hands and pointed out the falsehood in Dakota's accusation. "My hands aren't red," the Lizard said. "Neither are mine," the Frog stated. Then denials like, "Mine aren't either," came from the rest of the group.

It occurred to Dakota that this was an excellent opportunity to take advantage of the animals' ignorance and return to solving his own problem, so he began, after clearing his throat to gain their attention, "Because I did not participate, I should select the match. And I say that whoever finds a mask is the winner."

They all found this to be agreeable, for big, wobbly Dakota was a fair and just outsider, so he pulled out some coins from his pockets and said, "This is your reward. You may begin." When the creatures saw the money, they started being very nice to him. The Lizard and Frog licked his shoes and polished them. The Ferret picked up a few coins Dakota had emptied from his pockets earlier and presented them to him and said, "Pick me," which normally would have made Dakota laugh, except the Ferret was serious in his bribery. The White Mouse dove into the pool of money and, to Dakota's surprise, found an actual mask—it was in the face of a man who had a clothesline clip on either side to hold his cheeks back to form a forced smile.

Dakota announced the new victor and thought the matter was over, but the Black Rat started protesting that the title of champion had been stripped away from him because of the color of his fur. With a curious and sudden change of heart, the animals pitied the Rat and urged him to tell his struggle. And Dakota joined in the turn of events.

"Oh, dear Rat, when are you going to tell me your struggle?" Dakota asked very politely. "And if you feel quite all right to explain, please tell me the terrible things about flowers and cages, and so on."

Here the Black Rat settled down against the wall, and the others soon sat around him in a circle. "Every black rat faces the one and same struggle. Our experience be different. But only God can judge us," the Black Rat said in a tone of despair, then turned to the floor and sighed.

"I agree that God judges all of us," Dakota said, remembering what he had heard at church, then having failed to understand what the rodent meant, for everyone had their own challenges, he asked, "But why do you think your experience is so different from others?"

"Because I ain't never seen no land with no colorism," the Black Rat said. "It don't matter where I go. For example, one day, before I came to the New World, I was working for Residence for Rodents, building *nests* for—"

"*Vests*?" Dakota said.

"Dude, it be rude to interrupt." The Black Rat stared at him, and big, wobbly Dakota muttered a sorry. Then the rodent went on as before. "A new boss, a White English Mastiff, which I knew would be trouble from the start, took charge of our project. Not even half an hour had gone by when he pulled a yank-and-rank, called us in for our performance review. He took one good look at my black fur and sent me packing. 'Go back to the gutter where you belong!' That's what he said, and I was like, 'You for real?' He was wrong for that. Ain't even aks about my work. Colorism at its worst! Even in this day!"

Here the Black Rat paused with gloomy eyes and shook his head, then continued in an indignant voice. "What a rat supposed to do? A rat still got to eat, don't he? But the white devils deny us jobs and force us to stay in the ratchet sewer, and when we confront them for the wrongdoings they done did, all you be hearing is bogus apologies. So, we end up hustling." This was all very fascinating to Dakota, who once or twice wanted to say something but remained quiet to avoid being rude. "We ain't got no choice but to forage in gardens, foreign lands belonging to humans, but they be planting stinky flowers, like mines in a field, to keep us out. And if they catch us, you best believe we gonna be put in cages. Now you see what I'm saying?"

While the others consoled the Rat, the White Mouse gloated in his own little world, "We are superior." No one paid him any attention.

Dakota stepped back and said, still confused by the Rat's job, "You made vests? How curious! I would like to see you wear one."

"What else you want from me, man? Want me to put on tap shoes, get on the floor and dance? Want me to smile at you?" the Black Rat rebuked Dakota, then shook his head. "Keep on bad-mouthing."

"Oh, I'm sorry. I didn't mean to!" poor Dakota pleaded in a world of trouble again. "It's just that I've never seen a rat wear clothes, nor one that can dance—I would pay to see that!"

"All you see is color, you colorist!" the Black Rat snapped.

"Stop your colorism argument already, will you?" the Blue Frog said, which was followed by a bunch of *yeah*s.

"Some creatures wake up looking for problems," the Lizard commented to the Ferret, shaking his head. "It only takes one bad experience to generalize a whole group." And the Ferret agreed and pitied the Black Rat.

Dakota tucked his long hair behind his ears, as it kept getting in the way, and said rather upset, "And stop calling me names! You're lucky Bernie isn't here."

"Who's Bernie?" the Ferret asked.

"Bernie is my dog. He would've chased the Rat away. He has rescued me from squirrels whenever they have attacked me. And you should see how he manages other pests, lizards and frogs, and what not."

The crowd gasped and talked among themselves, then the White Mouse stepped up and said, "You let your dog chase creatures? Why, *you* are a colorist!"

The Black Rat gave Dakota a nasty gaze and said, "We all creatures at the end of the day. Don't judge us by what we look like but by who we are." He walked away without making so much as a noise while the others watched.

"Let's go back into the sewer, honey," the Green Lizard said to his wife, who had shed a tear, very distressed by the hate, and put his arm around her to comfort her.

"Come on children, this man is not good," the Brown Ferret said to his babies. "Not all humans are like this, but some are, and you should avoid such people."

"Some people are so poor, all they have is money," the Blue Frog said to the White Mouse, who agreed and started to go down the steps with the amphibian.

"How could they not like Bernie?" Dakota muttered to himself. "Everybody likes Bernie. He's the best dog in the world no matter what, and my best friend. Oh, Bernie, I will have to tell you all that has happened, that is, if we ever see each other again." And here Dakota sat down on the steps to the building and hung his head between his legs, dejected and confused. But in a short while, he raised his head at the sound of hurried footsteps and looked in the direction from which he thought they came, half hoping that the Black Rat would forgive him and let bygones be bygones.

Dakota and the American Dream

Chapter 5: The Squirrel reaches out to the Janitor

The Greenback Squirrel hurried out of the building and down the steps, and his eyes darted from one location to the next. Then he said to himself, "Where have my clubs and towel gone? They could be over here, over there—oh, I hope I didn't leave them in the barn, or worse, on the dooryard, where someone can budge them. Maybe I will have to buy a whole nother set." He viewed his Fitbit. "Oh, dear, my appointment is all set to start. Surely, the Bigwig will fire me before I can finish the rhyme, 'Adam Adler ate a lot of amazing acorns.'"

It occurred to Dakota that the bag the Squirrel was carrying earlier was really a golf bag with clubs in it, and he started to look around for the towel all the while wondering whether it would be a good idea to mention that he had used it.

"Mr. Bart," the fat Squirrel said in Dakota's direction.

Dakota looked over both his shoulders, one after the other, wondering who Mr. Bart was, but his search only turned up himself and the rodent.

Then the Squirrel shouted impatiently, "What on earth are you doing out here? Slacking off, eh? Go down to my office and get my clubs and towel. I must have left them there being that I'm in a hurry."

But Dakota only stood there, thoroughly confused.

"Go! Don't just stand there like some rookie!" The Squirrel pointed to the building.

Afraid of what the consequences might be, and not even having the presence of mind to correct the Squirrel, Dakota hastened into the building, strange and unsteady, for he was gravely thin having lost his water weight. In another moment the Buffalo rose from his chair to kick him out, so Dakota quickly snapped on the forced-smile mask, the one that the White Mouse had found, and the bison stopped and nodded in approval.

"Which way to the Greenback Squirrel's office?" he asked the Buffalo.

"Mister . . . it's right around the corner, to your left, sir."

Suddenly, big, wobbly Dakota did not at all like wearing the mask, for as the bison addressed him as "mister" and "sir," he forgot who he was and that was of course very frightening. However, Dakota hurried about, with his face turning sweaty under the mask, until finally he reached the office, where he slowed down and had the opportunity to think, quite astonished, "Has the Squirrel mistaken me for his worker? I should think not, but—why, I suppose he has!"

Next, Dakota took off the mask and tossed it aside. He viewed the door, which had white letters on the glass that read, "G. Squirrel," and chuckled because it sounded like an expression of surprise. In another moment he turned the knob and found himself outside again. It was a curious office, for there was a big, rectangular rock for a counter, grass for carpet, and the sky for the ceiling. Once the initial surprise went down, Dakota anxiously looked about for the golf gear and poked his head out every other minute or so, as the real Mr. Bart could appear any second.

"How strange it is," Dakota thought, "for a squirrel to be giving orders to a boy. Imagine Bernie doing the same. 'Dakota, come play fetch with me!' or 'Dakota, make me some apple chips,' or 'Dakota, pick up my poop.' Come to think of it, he already does that, except without the usual language."

After some time, not having found what he was looking for, Dakota ventured down a curvy hallway—a narrow passage formed by tall bushes on either side—with many doors, which gave him reason to worry that he were in some strange maze, and if he opened a door, there might be another passage with a set of doors, and it would go on like that forever, but when he opened a door, that was not the case and he relaxed. Instead, a messy room—closed off by tall bushes—with acorns everywhere showed itself. A log for a desk sat sideways on the grass, several books occupied a bookshelf—which was really a giant tree trunk that had been carved out—and in the corner, against the tall bushes, the golf bag rested, and with it, a pair of gloves.

In the next minute Dakota put the golf bag around his shoulder and heard a hissing from somewhere, but while he thought about where the curious sound came from, he searched through the drawers of the log desk for another towel. Just then his eyes chanced to fall upon a small paper box with the word "BARBERX" on it, and the phrase, "Reduces swelling of the hair," below that, in one of the compartments. Burning with curiosity, he opened the box and found a silver packet with several pills.

He pushed one pill out of the aluminum wrap and poured it into his palm. It was an elongated, cylindrical, red-white-and-blue striped pill with silver caps at each end of it that made the pill resemble a barber pole. "This must belong to the Squirrel. I think that explains his short fur," he said to himself, quite pleased with his determination. He imagined a squirrel without its medicine and had a little shriek of laughter: squirrels actually had very long fur and looked like hairballs. But when he returned to the box, there was a label on it which read, "For anyone with long hair. Dr. Quack." Here Dakota wondered if he'd ever meet this doctor, for he seemed to know a good deal about Dakota and his problems.

In another moment he turned the box over in his hand and found the directions: "Take this medicine with soda. Take one pill by mouth every long-hair day." And when he looked up, a chilled can of soda, along with a hand mirror, was sitting on the log desk, and he smiled to himself, not surprised in the least bit.

But before Dakota got all worked up for having found a solution to his long hair, which now had grown to his knees and made him feel like he was turning into a woman, he wondered whether he *could* take the medicine in the first place. He'd taken chewable vitamins before, even liquid medication, but never pills. He'd seen his mom and dad take pills, and certainly his grandparents, but they were hard to get down. He'd tried swallowing his vitamin before and it was no picnic.

Then it occurred to Dakota that perhaps his long hair was a side effect of the first medicine he had taken. He sighed, viewing the BARBERX pill before him. "I'm tired of this long hair. In any case it is itchy and there's so much of it that I wonder if something is living in it, like an owl. Mom would say I'm not presentable at all." Though there was the possibility of more side effects, Dakota couldn't bear the thought of his hair growing any longer, so he opened the sugary beverage and swallowed the pill with the soda.

The ease at which the pill went down surprised him, and he met his reflection in the mirror, waiting for something to happen.

Within seconds, his hair started to shorten and continued to do so until it became very small, maybe a quarter or half an inch, so he began to worry, "Why, if my hair keeps shrinking, I'll be completely bald!" Luckily for Dakota, the pill had finished its effect, and his hair stopped vanishing. Now his hair was short all around like that of a buzz cut. He turned his head one way, then the other, all the while observing his new look. "If I had just a little more hair, so that I could comb it, mom would say I look presentable—handsome!"

But soon his joints hurt, as though he were carrying extra weight, and he felt very tired. "Perhaps it's a side effect. Either that, or it is time for a nap." Dakota yawned and when he put his hand up to his mouth, his eyes fell upon his fingers, and he said, "But whatever am I going to do with these bony bones? Some water weight would be nice." For some minutes he went through the drawers, but no water was to be found, so he finished the can of soda, half hoping it might make his body wholesome again and give him some energy.

"These medicines are quite strong, indeed," poor Dakota thought. "Things were much better at home, where I was not always getting sick and having problems, like being too short to reach doorknobs, or having hair too long to manage. Oh, how I miss the days when I had a summer to enjoy, and my words didn't offend anyone, when money made me happy, and I didn't have to put on a mask. I wish I had never gotten a job in Corporate America, for it is very strange, and I wish there was an alternative, but everywhere I look, the buildings look the same as One Corporate Way."

Dakota looked over to the BARBERX box and sighed, then thought: "When I used to hear about grandma and grandpa having health problems, I fancied those things could never happen to me, and now here I am, having my own set of health problems. I'm a medical mystery—that I surely am. There should be a study done on me, that there should. And when I get back home, I'll visit a real doctor who could look at me and prescribe me medicine! But here I am already taking medicines and getting new problems all the time!"

Dakota pondered the paradox of taking medicine yet turning sick another way all the while forgetting the golf gear and his duties to the

Greenback Squirrel. "But could there be a wonder drug so that I never have to visit a doctor again? That would be a sign of good medicine, indeed. One way, to never have to take shots, or bitter medicine, or wait for a doctor, but then, to always have to be in school—no sick days for me—and not having colorful Band-Aids to wear and suckers to suck on! Oh, I wouldn't want to miss out on that!"

"Oh, you stupid child, how can you miss school here? There is only work. And how can you have a nice Band-Aid or sucker? Why, there isn't even a doctor here. Just some Quack!"

He went on weighing both sides of there being a wonder drug, thinking of the pros, then the cons, and counting each side and getting lost every so often, until after some minutes he heard a familiar voice from outside the office.

"Mr. Bart! Mr. Bart!" streaked through the passage between the tall bushes. "Where are my golf clubs, my towel?" Then the pattering of feet came, louder and louder, as did the voice, which seemed to address someone else. "You're going the wrong way. Bang a u-ey, get on the rotary, take Route 7 to—if there's a gawker blocker, get on the Pike! Quarter of ten, and you'll be down at the golf club."

Suddenly, Dakota filled up with worry, though he had found all the items requested by the Squirrel, even another towel in one of the drawers.

In another minute the fat Squirrel entered the room. He put away a banana—his version of a phone—in his pocket and gaped before saying in a puzzled voice, "Who are you?"

"Why, I'm Dak—" Dakota checked himself before he let it be known who he really was, then ventured to say, "I'm Mr. Bart, of course, and I've got your bag and towel right here, sir." He held up the towel, then turned to show the bag around his shoulder.

"You're not Mr. Bart. You look nothing like him," the Squirrel said in a decided tone, then put his hand up high. "He's tall and has got long hair, and he's not big around the waist!"

It never occurred to Dakota while he was busy taking one side over another that he had shrunk to half his height, and his belly had grown wide so that he was chubby and husky at the same time—chusky. "How did that ever happen?" he said to himself. In the next moment he wondered if the instructions on the box—"for anyone with long hair"—really were for the Squirrel, and squirrels were actually giant creatures that had turned small and fat after taking BARBERX.

Dakota and the American Dream

"You're an impostor!" the Squirrel persisted, pointing at him.

"No, no, I'm the same person, indeed. It's just—" Dakota pleaded. He made up his mind that it might not serve him well to explain how things happened, for he was not sure how to begin. "I'm your worker, Mr. Bart, and I got what you wanted."

"If you are in fact Mr. Bart, then tell me, what do you do here?"

"Well, I, you see, it is, well, I work and, and—"

"Your job is to do whatever I tell you, that's it!"

"Yes, I was going to say that in any case. Oh, Greenback Squirrel, please believe me. I'm the same person, or I think I am," Dakota said doubtfully, not sure whether he was the same person as before, being that he had gone through so many changes.

"Well, then, if you are my worker, I am displeased with your work." The Squirrel took a pink sticky note from his log table and handed it to Dakota. "It is time for you to go."

At first Dakota thought he'd ask, "What's this for?" but then it occurred to him that the Squirrel only gave orders to be followed, so he took the initiative to say, "What would you like me to do with this, sir?"

"Take a Dudley! That's what," the Squirrel said furiously and pointed to the doorway.

"Oh, but I really do want to work here. I have hardly got a chance to show you what I can do. And I know so many wonderful things, and I'm very good at learning."

"The pink slip has spoken," the Squirrel said in a decided tone. He crossed his arms and glared at Dakota as he waited for him to leave.

Dakota looked at the pink slip and wondered how such a small, colored paper that he might use in art class had so much power to say whether he could work or not. He ventured to tear up the paper and let the pieces fall upon the grass.

"Want to go? Want to go?" the Squirrel said indignantly, rolling up his sleeves.

Dakota did not at all want to get into a scuffle with the creature, so he said in an apologetic tone, "Dear Squirrel, I'm very sor—"

But the Squirrel would hear nothing of it and screamed with passion, toward the doorway, "Josefina! Josefina! Clean this mess!"

No sooner did he finish than a hurried, rough voice responded, "Coming, *señor*, coming!"

Dakota waited for some time without hearing much. Then at last came a squeaky, rumbling set of wheels from a cart, with the sound of equipment banging against the plastic and a few mixed voices all talking among themselves, from down the passage between the tall bushes.

"*Dame la* broom *y* dustpan, Josefina!—I left them *en la última oficina*!—Never mind that! I will run and get it—Yes, you go on and do that, *mientras preparo los* mops *y el* bucket—That *es una gran idea*! And what will you do, Josefina?—Well, I'll take this cart *a la oficina* the Big Boss needs us at and clean up the mess—Empty *la papelera y* put a new bag in it, will you?—Why don't you take care of that matter? *Tengo que* tear loose some towels *y abrir esta* tissue box—Very well then, I'll do that. *Pero quién preparará los* cleaning supplies?—I suppose I could do it, *ya que todavía no tengo una tarea.*"

"Poor Josefina," Dakota said to himself. "Why, she can't even speak English! These pieces of paper, which shouldn't take more than a few seconds I gather, should be the least of her worries. I wouldn't want to be in her position. Why, she doesn't know the language and instead speaks some invention between Spanish and English—Spanglish!"

"Now, which way *es esa oficina* we need to be at?" Josefina asked in a puzzled voice. "*No tengo la menor idea*. It could be any one of these."

The Greenback Squirrel stepped out for a moment and waved. "Yoo-hoo! Yoo-hoo! Down here, janitors. I have one small mess that needs cleaning"—then he glanced at Dakota—"and one nasty pest that needs removing!"

"How rude!" In a furious passion Dakota slammed the door on the Squirrel and locked him out. The rodent banged on the door, and Dakota wondered what he would do now. "Oh, mind your temper, Dakota. Look what mess you've got yourself into."

"Open this door right this minute! Or I'll reach out to the boys!"

"And I'll reach out to Bernie!"

That cooled the Squirrel. He was silent until the squeaky wheels of the janitorial cart came to a halt. "What are they going to do?" Dakota thought, terribly frightened. He pressed his ear up against the door and listened to the voices outside.

"Where is the mess, *señor*?"—"It's right in there, but that pest I spoke about has locked us out"—"If it is alive, you will have to call *al exterminador*"—"I'm empowering you with more duties for the moment. You are promoted and can now remove pests when they appear"—"*Gracias señor. Pero no tengo* training *y no sé cómo* remove pests"—"It is on-the-job training, so get in there and do your dirty work!"—"*Pero señor*"—"Do as I say, or I'll have you fired!"

Next came a clinking of keys, and Dakota kept his hand on the doorknob, for he was certain they would attempt to open the door. In another moment they began trying keys one by one with Josefina saying, "No, it's not that one. Let's try *otro*." And they went on in this way, trying several keys until they came upon the right one, but Dakota locked the door as soon as they unlocked it, so they reasoned that it wasn't the right one and continued. "*Bueno*, that is the last of them," she said.

"Get out, you big mess!" the Squirrel screamed with passion, then in a whisper, "Grab some. When he comes out, stuff him in the barrel."

"Grab what?" Dakota thought. But he only had a short while to guess what they were taking hold of, for a can of cleaner suddenly came flying at him from above. "Watch where you're throwing things!" he screamed, having never seen such workplace violence. "I could have been hit!" He approached the bushes surrounding the door and squinted as he looked through them; the animals, now exposed, included a Skunk and a Wolverine wearing janitorial uniforms and standing on their hind legs among other stinky creatures.

In another minute a storm of office supplies came crashing down on poor Dakota, and he ducked with some difficulty, being that he had become short and fat, and hid under the log desk where you normally put your feet. When he knelt down, his eyes chanced to fall upon a curious trapdoor in the grass, and he made an attempt to open it, but it was locked. So he curled himself up into a ball and waited, buried in worry and not sure what to do.

After they had run out of office supplies to throw at him, the animals started throwing the keys. Dakota stared at them with some amusement as they collected on the grass. Just then a brilliant idea came to him: perhaps one of the keys could open the trapdoor under the log desk. "If I find the right key, I'm sure to get out of here!"

So he reached over and tried key after key, and was delighted to find that he had found the right match after a few attempts. He crawled into the dark space—it was like a rabbit hole for adults—and shut the trapdoor behind him, then went on for a little way until he came upon another similar door. As soon as he exited the crawl space, he wound up outside under another log desk and, seeing that he was surrounded by tall bushes once more, exclaimed, "Why, I must be in another office!"

Dakota stood and, upon looking all around him, met a door. In another moment he opened it and found himself in a passage. He began on his way but soon heard arguing from the animals who tried to force him out of the office, and when he turned the corner, he saw the Greenback Squirrel putting a clothesline clip on his nose and saying to the Skunk, "You're skeeving us out, Josefina!" as all the creatures became surrounded by green gas.

Seeking to avoid another clash, Dakota turned back and hurried in the opposite direction. Soon he became tired, for he was chusky, and walked. Once he had gone a good way, turning corners and moving around curves, he began to plot his next steps.

"First things first," Dakota said, "I must tie my shoes, or else I might trip. Secondly, I must find my way out of this maze and to the top of this building. I'm sure if I can manage to get out of here, my plan will work."

And it was a splendid plan, except that when Dakota tried to bend over and tie his shoe laces, he found that he could only make it halfway there. He pushed and pushed for some time, but only made standing crunches with an upset face. At last he gave up and sighed. However, being ever so crafty, wise Dakota imagined, "Well, I may not be able to bend over, but I'm sure there is a set of chopsticks somewhere, perhaps in Asia, that a dragon or sumo wrestler once used, that I could take advantage of to tie my shoes. It'll be just like picking up noodles, big noodles." He smiled with delight, having found a clever way.

In the next moment he began to mime the action of using the giant chopsticks, as though he already possessed them, but he soon became discouraged. "Oh, who am I kidding? I don't even know how to use regular chopsticks. How am I ever going to use those for dragons and sumo wrestlers?"

Here Dakota began to walk very carefully, so as to not trip and hurt himself, and went on thinking how he would manage to tie his shoes until he came upon an open doorway standing alone without a wall. He approached the opening with great delight, for the space beyond it looked like the lobby where the bison was, but suddenly, his belly swelled, so much that he was now more than four feet in diameter, and pressed against the bushes on both sides. "Holy seeds, I've really ballooned in size! Whatever am I going to do now? I'll never make it to the other side, never!"

In spite of that, Dakota tried to go through the doorway. He pushed with all his might but only wound up stuck in the doorframe. Oh, to look through and be teased by his dreams of reaching the top was painful. But to get from one side to the other was hopeless. His face became upset with discomfort as he stood there sweating, and it occurred to him that this weight was not that of water, for he didn't reduce in circumference as he did before.

"I think this is a side effect of the last medicine, indeed. Anyway, you should be ashamed of yourself," Dakota said severely, "a good boy like you to turn into a ball! Stop growing fatter this moment, I order you!" Here he looked down in despair and suddenly found his feet to have disappeared, hidden beneath his roundness. As he continued to press against the doorframe, it occurred to him that he just might break the doorway, and in the next moment, as he pushed forward, short, supersized Dakota popped out at last and rolled like a ball for a good while before crashing into a wall.

Luckily for Dakota, he was not hurt in the least bit (for, you see, the fat acted like a cushion and softened the blow). "Oh, this is a curious day indeed," Dakota thought. "It is unlike any other, for I don't think I've met one like this before, not even in my dreams. All I remember was going to the park, and now I'm somewhere entirely different and someone other than myself. But if I'm not myself, then who am I?"

Here Dakota began to think of who he had become, if it were actually possible to become someone other than oneself. He did want to be a fireman at one point, then a pilot, but he hadn't turned into either of them. And though he admired famous people and wanted to be like a few of them, he wasn't like any of his idols. So he started to believe that he might have changed into a friend at school and went one by one comparing himself to his friends.

"I can't be Sanjay," he said in a solemn tone, "for he is tall, very strange, and I'm not, at least not anymore. And there is no way I'm Madison, seeing that I don't have long hair, and I'm not a girl. And I'm certainly not Chuck—or, as everyone else calls him, Chubs—for I can still do all sorts of activities, and he, oh, he can't and doesn't do anything but sits all day like a couch potato! Plus, he, he and I, we're not the same because I'm healthy."

But worry and doubt surfaced within Dakota's poor, fat heart, so he did his best to push them down. "I know that I'm not Chubs, for I can still get up by myself and run." Here Dakota tried to get up but struggled very much and needed the support of the wall. When he at last rose to his feet, he said, "There must be an elevator here somewhere," and as he began, he found that he couldn't jog without losing his breath, much less run.

"Oh, never mind running. I can jump high, and Chubs cannot." Dakota bent his knees and pushed up, but he wasn't sure whether he left the ground, for his feet felt as though they had stayed on the tile. He tried again but met the same result.

"I can't even jump. Holy seeds, who have I become? None other than Chubs!" Dakota wondered how he had changed overnight to become everything his mother warned him not to become. He had taken steps to avoid growing heavy, like playing at recess and participating in gym class. Just then a brilliant idea came to his mind, and he said in an encouraging tone, "I'll sing 'Head, Shoulders, Knees and Toes' and show myself that I'm not Chubs at all." So Dakota brought his brows together in a determined look and started.

"Head, shoulders, knees, knees, knees—"

Now of course Dakota touched his head and shoulders, but he never once made it to his knees, quite forgetting in his haste that he could not bend over. Then he gave it another go.

"Head, shoulders, knees, knees, knees—"

"I'm sure I could reach my knees and toes if I removed my jacket," short, supersized Dakota cried, half hoping that he hadn't lost his childish flexibility. Of course his next attempt proved to be a failure, and his eyes welled up with tears. "I am Chubs, and I shall go on being teased at school for bringing three lunchboxes, and need a special chair, because I can't fit into any of the normal chairs, and watch the other children jump and dance and run and play during recess!"

Here poor Dakota began to cry and feel terrible, but in a minute or two, he said, "Well that settles that, I am indeed Chubs. Come, there's no use in weeping like that. I shall go back into the maze, for if I stay there, then I won't have to face the children at school. And if my family comes to get me, I'll tell my parents to talk to my teachers, so that I won't be teased at school for being very fat. I do hope they come get me; I am so tired of all these curious changes!"

While he was lamenting the way he looked and comforting himself, a little meow just above his head made his gaze turn up in a moment's notice.

A giant kitten was standing on its hind legs, peering into a large window high above, while leaning on the wall and scratching at it. "Holy seeds," Dakota said in a shrill voice, then called after it, "Hello, Kitty!" Just then he became terribly frightened, for it occurred to him that this was no small pussy to play with. And if it were clawing at the wall, trying to get whatever was behind the window, heaven only knows what it might do to poor Dakota, a boy the size of a mouse compared to it.

At this the Kitty set its eyes on Dakota and came down on all fours with stiffened rear legs and a raised rear end. The cat stared and growled at short, supersized Dakota, and he went weak in the knees. But wise Dakota had the presence of mind to anticipate what the cat might do, so when the pussy took a swipe at him, he luckily dodged its paw and scurried away as hard as he could go. Soon he turned a corner and found himself standing before a giant ball of rubber bands.

The cat meowed, and its shadow grew as it pursued him. He went behind the ball of rubber bands and pushed it out in front; on which the Kitty jumped onto the ball, with a shriek of delight, and followed the plaything as it slipped away from its claws. Dakota slowly managed to slip past the cat all the while keeping an alert gaze on the pussy. The Kitty chased the ball in the space ahead and in the next moment seemed to have a game of play, for it charged at the ball, one way, then the other. It was indeed a good time to escape, so once Dakota caught his breath, he turned the corner from where he came and peeked to see how the cat was doing. To Dakota's surprise the Kitty had tumbled over and become entangled in the ball of rubber bands.

Dakota put his hand to his mouth and chuckled as the cat meowed repeatedly. After a minute or two, he set off to the top of the skyscraper. "It would be nice to have a cat, though not as big as that," Dakota said as he waddled back and forth like a penguin down the hallway, looking about for an elevator. "Bernie would chase her, and the kitty would scream, like children playing 'tag, you're it!'"

Soon Dakota came upon a restroom and settled on a plan of action to go in and make sure his appearance had not changed for the worse, for he was becoming quite used to the fact that unsightly changes occurred without his knowing. He found himself standing on dirt, outside again, and approached a curious tree which had a mirror on its trunk, just above a wooden sink. The mirror was covered in spots so that it looked as though somebody had brushed their teeth in front of it; nevertheless, the looking glass showed his reflection.

"Holy seeds! Whatever happened to my face?" Dakota cried in a shrill and passionate voice. Tiny bumps and redness extended over it, and he put his hand up and touched his face, for he had never seen such a thing. "I think I have acne! The older children warned me this day would come, but I never thought it would happen so soon. Oh, how will I ever manage this? There must be some medicine for it, but what?"

Poor Dakota looked all around him to see if any more cough syrup bottles or small boxes with medicine in them appeared, but Dr. Quack had not provided any syrup, or pills, or whatever else you might find in a pharmacy. So Dakota returned to the looking glass and said, "Come, there's no use in worrying. I'm sure I'll grow too big for acne one day, just like mom and dad." Here he began to smile, relieved that all the bumps and redness would last only a short while, except that when he did so, the mirror showed a most hideous reflection.

"Whenever did my teeth become so crooked?" He shook his head, half in shock, half in fear. "Now I will have to get braces." Suddenly, teenage Dakota looked away from his image and to another area of the looking glass. When he narrowed his eyes on the back of the mirror, water began to go down it like a waterfall and in another moment his reflection disappeared.

At this he moved closer so that his nose nearly touched the strange looking glass, and his eyes looked about for an explanation because normal mirrors didn't misbehave or act out like this. After a minute or two, the water stopped flowing and a set of brown eyes appeared, then a nose, which was followed by a mouth, chewing gum of all things, and the most curious part was that it wasn't a person behind the mirror, but a mask.

Dakota and the American Dream

Chapter 6: The Mask in the Looking Glass

The mask was made of porcelain and had pink cheeks, matching eye shadow, and rosy lips. A black birdcage veil hung over its brown eyes and a white-and-black headband with white and black feathers sat above its pencil-thin eyebrows. Dakota stared at the strange mask for some time as it blew a great bubble with the gum. At last the bubble popped all over its face, and a gloved hand with no arm appeared from below and wiped the gum off.

"Do you look beautiful today?" the Mask in the Looking Glass asked in a female voice before putting the gum back into her mouth.

This was not a question teenage Dakota wanted to face, for he didn't have a pleasant response. So he replied in a timid voice, "I—I hardly know what to say, for this mirror is playing tricks on me! I'm a young, handsome man and what do I see? Not me!"

"Tricks? What do you mean by that?" she said in an offended tone. "Please tell me."

"I can't, because only a magic mirror knows how it does what it does. There is something curious about you."

"I'm not broken, nor am I covered in dust, so it can't possibly be me. Therefore, it must be you. And to remedy that you should be clearer."

"I'm afraid I can't because I'm not a mirror," Dakota said in a melancholy tone. "I have changed in appearance so many times and without control that it is quite troubling—no, depressing."

51

"Depressing? Not at all," the Mask in the Looking Glass said in an encouraging tone. "Why, every change is a chance to begin afresh and make yourself the way you wish."

"Well, you may not think so," Dakota argued, very gloomy, "but when you have to look at yourself in the mirror—someone will put a mirror in front of you one day—and then after that you'll see your spots, your blemishes, I think you'll be depressed, won't you?"

"I couldn't care less," she said quite confidently.

"Well, you might reflect and reason to yourself that it's okay, not depressing," Dakota went on, "but in any case, when I stare at the man in the mirror, I'd like to see some changes."

"Yes, you *do* need to make changes, though not the ones you think," the Mask in the Looking Glass said. "Tell me, what is beauty?"

"Well, I can't because I don't recall a time when I felt confident about my image. I think you should stop judging me, for I do that to myself quite too much."

"You do!" she said sharply. "But what is beauty?"

Here teenage Dakota began to have an unpleasant temper about him, for he did not at all like being asked this question. In another moment Dakota boiled over and cried loudly.

"Now, now, don't *wail*—"

"I'm not a *whale*!" Dakota shouted. "You don't have to call me names."

"Oh, dear . . ." the porcelain face said, rolling her eyes.

"I don't have to take this kind of harassment." He stuck his tongue out and stormed away in a furious passion.

"Wait!" she called after him. "I'm not out to get you. I have something good to say that will make you feel better about yourself."

Dakota suddenly stopped and thought, "Come, there's no use in getting worked up like this." And he came back in a grudging sort of way, hoping the Mask in the Looking Glass would be nice to him this time around.

"My, my, you do get upset in a hurry," she remarked.

"That does not make me feel better," Dakota said at once.

"It was not meant to." The Mask in the Looking Glass began to blow a bubble again.

Teenage Dakota waited politely at first, but as the bubble ballooned for some minutes, he became impatient with the porcelain face and thought, "How rude, having me wait for it. I wish it would stop doing that."

Before long the bubble popped over the sculptured face, and she collected the gum back in her mouth and said, "So, you can't face the man in the mirror?"

"I'm afraid I can't," Dakota said in a sorrowful tone. "I can't stand the sight of me as I used to, and I don't fancy the changes I've been through, strange and tall, fat and bald, acne and all." His head turned down, and he remarked, very gloomy, "Nothing seems to give me joy."

"Nothing?" she asked.

"Well, I've tried exercising—singing and dancing at the same time—and I know exercise can make one feel better, but I can't quite do it anymore."

"Forget about exercising for the moment," the Mask in the Looking Glass ordered. "Maybe a good song by itself would cheer you up. Sing 'I Look in the Mirror' by the Wiggles. You do know that song, don't you?"

"Don't be ridiculous, of course I do," Dakota said at once. Then he turned away from the melancholy thoughts of his self-image to his pleasant voice. He put his hand on his stomach—let it rise and fall— and started to sing from there, as he had been instructed in school.

"I look in the mirror and what do I see?
Two chins laughing at me
They sit there unhappy, and I can see
There's no one in the world as ugly as me

I look in the mirror and what do I see?
One big tummy sticking out at me
I stuff it with everything everyday
And there's no one fatter than me I say

I look in the mirror and what do I see?
One terrible frown frowning straight at me
My teeth need braces definitely, and I can see
There's no one in the world as ugly as me

I look in the mirror and what do I see?
One crater face looking out at me

53

I feel so sad that I'm here today
And there's no one as sad as me I say
There's no one as ugly as me I say."

At the end of the nursery rhyme, Dakota sunk into a deep despair and thought, very ashamed, "Applesauce! I couldn't have changed from having a baby face to having a crater face—a nice, healthy boy to a fat dough boy."

"You have forgotten the words, or you have forgotten what joy comes from music. Either way, that didn't sound good," the Mask in the Looking Glass said.

"Not good at all, I'm afraid," Dakota remarked and fell to silent brooding. After a minute or two, he said, "I know the words, but my heart is not in them."

"Yes, you have lost all feeling, all passion," she observed, "and it shows in everything you do." Then she began to blow a bubble again, but when it grew to half its potential, the porcelain face took it back in and said, rather sternly, "Looks aren't everything. Your appearance is only a reflection of what you put in. You are what you eat, don't you agree?"

"Well, I haven't had much to put in, only some medicine and soda, but that, I should think, couldn't have done this to me."

"Why not? *Everything* has a side effect," the Mask in the Looking Glass said very wisely.

"Yes, well, I suppose it does," Dakota agreed reluctantly. Just then it occurred to him that with every action he took, there was always a chance that something bad might happen, a new problem might arise. He had only to look for a solution before he wound up with some trouble, and as terrible as that was, the cycle would continue.

"Tell me, how would you like to look?"

"Oh, I don't have much of a preference," Dakota said, "except that everything and everyone around me tells me I should look a certain way, that I should be a certain way to be considered handsome, and that is what depresses me. Does that make sense?"

The Mask in the Looking Glass started blowing another bubble, and Dakota sighed and half hoped for the bubble to pop and make a mess. Before long the sculptured face gathered the gum in her mouth and said without sympathy, "It is what it is," which only made Dakota feel worse, for he suddenly found himself on an island of his own, and in another moment he became angry.

"Are you content with your image today?" the porcelain face asked.

"Well, no, I am not," Dakota replied. "I would like to have muscles, but not too many, and be tall, but not too much, and have a full head of hair, but not so long, and have straight teeth, not all these crooked things, and have a clear face, none of this redness. Being round and having all these marks on my face is ugly."

"The size and spots are perfect—flawless!" she said in an offended tone, furrowing her brows (for, you see, the Mask in the Looking Glass was round and appeared to have blemishes on its face because the mirror had water stains on the surface).

"But it doesn't fancy me," teenage Dakota pleaded with pity, then thought, "I wish you'd understand."

"You'll learn to love yourself in time," the Mask in the Looking Glass said in a soothing tone and started to blow a bubble again.

Just then water began to run down the looking glass, and Dakota asked in a trembling voice, "Where . . . where are you going?" In another moment the water stopped flowing and the porcelain face disappeared altogether. Poor Dakota stretched his hand out to the mirror and ventured to touch it.

"Don't do that!" the porcelain face said severely but faintly, as though she had gone very far. "You'll make smudges, and I'll look ugly!" she mocked in a whiny voice. In the silence that followed, Dakota anxiously looked about in the looking glass for the mask, but only met his wretched appearance. So he backed away, and in the next moment a small object like a lipstick tube came flying out from the mirror, and he juggled the item before grabbing hold of it.

"Dr. Quack's order," the porcelain face said in the same echoing voice. "It'll give you the power, the lure of beauty, but I warn you, it's dangerous."

At this Dakota turned to the object that had been thrown to him. "Why, it's an inhaler!" He had seen a boy at school use one whenever his asthma flared up. He looked thoughtfully at the inhaler and read the label. "Sveltezac. Take three puffs every depressing moment of the day. Patient may experience unwanted attention." Here Dakota paused to worry, "Oh, whatever will happen to dear me if I take this medicine? So many out-of-the-way things have happened that they seem not out-of-the-way at all! Come, there's no use in being afraid. A big boy like you should have courage." He ventured to take the medicine and followed the instructions: shake the inhaler for some time, put it up to your mouth, and breathe in as you press the inhaler.

Soon a curious stirring rose in his body that began in his stomach and reached out to the ends of his fingers and toes, and in the next moment his appearance started to change. First, hair grew on his head, brushed up at the front like Elvis and gelled to perfection, as though he had a professional stylist shape his hair. Then his jaw became square, his teeth turned straight, his cheek bones grew high, and his nose turned sharp, so that his whole face carried a symmetry that he'd never seen before.

"My hair is just right at last!" Dakota said with great delight. Now he had to take two more puffs; he wasted no time and repeated the steps.

Next came a broadening of the shoulders and a toning of the arms. Suddenly, his shoulders dipped back, his chest jutted forward, and his tummy tucked so that there was no more fat, just muscle. The last inhalation made his legs sturdy and his body strong all over. By the time he had finished evolving, he was an entirely different being— presentable and attractive as he had wanted.

"I've never looked this good, never! My appearance is perfectly handsome," Dakota remarked, then touching his face, "And oh, my face, how clear and fair it is." His doubts were cut asunder, except there was a shred of worry that his new look might not last. "I wish I remain forever young and handsome."

Of course he had to test his new body; he tried to jump and in another moment said, very gladly, "Why, I can jump as high as a kangaroo!" When he came down, he ventured to bend over and touch his toes. "Holy seeds, I can reach the floor!" He hurried out of the restroom and into the hallway with the plan of sprinting to wherever the elevator was, except a shill cry of excitement stopped him before he could so much as pass the Kitty tangled in the ball of rubber bands: a donkey on its hind legs wearing a dull gray business dress approached while looking him up and down.

"Hey, stallion!" the donkey exclaimed in a peculiar female accent.

"Hello," Dakota greeted politely. "Can you please tell me how to get to the top?"

"I'm Jenny from Alabama, and I have found me something slap-your-mama-good! Ooh, I'm nervous as a long-tailed cat in a room full of rocking chairs!" the jenny said in a thrilled tone, then added with a wishful voice, "It's been a hot minute since I've seen a stallion. I've been hankering for one and tried everything, but they're always too uppity for me!"

"Huh? I don't have the slightest idea what you mean," Dakota said very nicely.

"I've tried flirting with them and done everything to not look ugly as sin—putting on make-up, doing my hair, my nails, getting tans—and I've even tried dressing like a floozy," Jenny continued, without any mind to her chatter, "but all I get is some horse who fell out the ugly tree—horseface! No stallions, save for one time. They're hard to please. I don't know what it takes to be with y'all."

Dakota was thoroughly puzzled, and when he raised his hand to stop her, she went on, babbling away in her own little world.

"As if it isn't hard enough for a girl to make it on her own," the jenny said. "I'm tuckered out from chasing y'all, but I keep on trying. Keep on looking for that one guy, not any guy, the right guy, to make little hinnies with." She covered her mouth with her hoof, a humanlike hand. "Ooh, I'm counting chickens before they hatch!"

"I'm sorry you haven't met this perfect man," Dakota said politely, now starting to understand that she fancied him. "But do you know where the elevator is?"

"And just when I reckon I've found the right one," Jenny said in a melancholy tone, "and just when I reckon we had chemistry, they leave me. Ugh, what is with y'all?"

"But I'm not a stallion," Dakota argued. "I'm—"

"Oh, you're just being modest. I like that! But you are in fact one, and you can't hide it!" Jenny said.

"I'm just a boy, or *was*," Dakota said in a timid voice, as he wasn't quite sure if he really was that anymore with all the changes he'd been through. Handsome Dakota began to wonder how to end the conversation, and suddenly an extraordinary excuse came to him, so he at once said, "And I shouldn't speak to strangers."

"You're sweet, and I reckon that you're playing hard-to-get," Jenny said in a flirty tone. "I've been with your kind before, but never with one as perfect as you! Your hair and face, your size and shape.

You're a stallion, as rare as rocking horse manure, and I say flaunt it if you got it. But I reckon you'll tell me that I'm not your type."

"Well, you're not my type at all," Dakota said as a matter of fact, "being that I'm a little boy and little boys shouldn't talk to strangers." (He thought of himself as a little boy, for, you see, though he had undergone several physical changes, he was still a child at heart.)

"Why are y'all slow as molasses, dumb as a box of rocks?" Jenny said rather emphatically. "You don't sound like a stud when you open your mouth. Why don't you just walk around with a sign stuck to your head that says, 'I'm a colt.' What is the point of making yourself out to be fine wine and wasting a girl's time?"

The whole idea of walking around with a sign attached to his forehead was new to Dakota, so he imagined the scene but for only a moment, as the jenny had more to add.

"You're too big for your britches, I can see that now, but as long as you have that figure, it doesn't matter to me whether you're an immature colt or a stallion!" She looked about her purse, then brought out a small card. "I'm fixing to go back to work, but here's my number."

"I don't want your number," Dakota said angrily and pushed her hand away. "I'm not interested in jennies, and even if I was, I wouldn't want to be with you!"

"Ooh, you were raised in a barn, talking uppity like that. When you're looking for something serious, holler at me, maybe?" Jenny said in a stern yet hopeful tone as she walked past him.

As Dakota watched her leave, a vending machine came into view, and he waited until the jenny was out of sight, then approached the snack dispenser. A curious bag of chips hung alone in the center, and he dug into his pockets and of course found some change. Dakota inserted the coins and pressed the right buttons, then gathered the bag and tucked it away in his pocket for later. Next, he went the opposite direction and tried to put the strange interaction with the jenny out of his head as best he could, for his child's mind kept getting caught up in the argument, and every now and then he had to shake his head to get free from his thoughts.

After a minute or two, it occurred to handsome Dakota that he could avoid unwanted attention—a curious side effect of Sveltezac—if he changed his appearance, and that might be possible with the mask the White Mouse had given him. Oh, how he wished he hadn't thrown

Sameer Garach

it away. In another moment a new idea emerged: the makeover he sought rested in the bag of chips. So he set to make himself different at once, thinking junk food might do the trick.

He popped open the bag very loudly and smiled—no teacher was around to tell him not to make a noise—then ventured to take a small bite of a chip, careful not to take in too much, as he had no desire to become fat again but hoped to grow enough to prevent jennies from throwing themselves so loosely at him.

In another moment his nose turned fairly fat, just as he had thought it would, and wanting to thicken some more, he finished the chip and ate a few more. Soon his belly grew a little way, and he looked like an average man for once, slightly filled out and kind of tall, not showing off and not falling behind. For once, junk food came in handy, and he learned that perhaps it was not so bad if it were taken in moderation.

It had been so long since he'd been anything but average, where he thought he should be as an adult, that it felt unusual to begin with. But he found himself glad with it before long, a sort of self-love he had been missing for quite some time. "I wish I don't have any more problems," he thought, "for I am tired of the curious things medicine and junk food can do to me! I seem normal for the time being, and oh, how I expect to stay that way if I have nothing more. Now I must find a way to the top of the building, except I don't know where to start!"

Just then a round glass door ahead showed a courtyard behind it, and he went there at once and found himself standing directly under the sun in an enclosed, square area with patio furniture—tables and chairs under umbrellas held by, of all curious things, elephants. A peculiar coffeehouse with a glass tree appeared standing a way off at the corner opposite him. "Holy seeds, I've never seen a coffee shop like this, never! And seeing that I'm the right size to not attract any creatures, I haven't the slightest hesitation to ask someone there for directions!"

Dakota and the American Dream

Chapter 7: Cracker and Coffee

Average-sized Dakota hesitated to approach the coffeehouse, as he was more interested in a large fountain and waterfall just in front of it in the center of the courtyard; a Mermaid with flowing brown hair lay on top of a rock in the middle of the pool. Suddenly, a grainy creature rose out of the water, dripping sand and wearing a dull gray suit jacket, and stood on its tail.

"Holy seeds, a shark made of sand!" Dakota thought.

The Sand Shark pulled out a conch shell from within and blew it very loudly at the Mermaid, who hadn't noticed the creature until now, as she was busy sunbathing.

The Mermaid sat up at once and shoved the conch shell down the Shark's throat, splashing sand everywhere. "You didn't have to do that!" she said in a voice of thunder.

"And you didn't have to do *that*!" The Sand Shark readjusted the sand so that his figure returned to normal.

Dakota became curious to see the happenings and ventured to crouch behind an elephant carefully, half afraid that he would upset it, half hoping he wouldn't, and listened in secret.

The Sand Shark again reached within himself, produced a little oyster, and handed it to the Mermaid. She opened the oyster and found a small card and proceeded to read it aloud. "The Board of Directors and Big Boss cordially invites the Bigwig and her assistant, Mermaid, to participate in the Creature Company Tournament to be held at the Country Club Golf Course in the New World, the twenty-sixth of April.

Chairman." The Mermaid put the card away, tossed the oyster into the fountain, and said in a peculiar accent, "The Bigwig is already aware, but I can't speak for her; she thinks who she is. And as for me—" She pulled out a circular sea shell from her sting ray handbag and flipped through the ridges, as though the sea shell were a Rolodex, or circular index of cards, searching for something.

Average-sized Dakota found all her things amusing and started to come out from behind the elephant to get a closer look but suddenly checked himself, for he remembered to stay back and not interfere.

"How unfortunate!" the Mermaid remarked with an insincere voice and glanced away from her sea shell to the Sand Shark. "I can't make it because I have a *shell-abration* to attend."

"That's nothing but a lame pun, a lame excuse, to avoid a company event—a team-building exercise," the Sand Shark said rather pointedly.

"A lame pun? Maybe. A sick passenger? Of course not," the Mermaid said coolly.

"It is an invitation from the Big Boss. You must come," the Sand Shark snapped.

The Mermaid yawned. "I will do my best. That's a fact."

"You will come! Otherwise you will not be promoted to a full woman and will remain a half-woman, half-fish." Suddenly, the Sand Shark leapt at her, and she dove into the water. The Sand Shark followed her, right on her tail, as she jumped into and out of the water repeatedly and screamed "fins" every time she surfaced, and they made quite a mess, splashing water everywhere. Dakota covered his mouth to make sure they didn't hear his little shriek of laughter.

Then the Mermaid returned to the rock and cried, "Ugh, I hate it here. Whatsamattaferu?"

"Very well then," the Sand Shark said. "Don't expect to be promoted. This was your chance!" In another moment the Sand Shark vanished just as he had come.

The Mermaid lay down, faced the sky, and closed her eyes. Dakota tiptoed toward her, then proceeded in the same way to pass her and head to the coffee shop, where he might get an opportunity to taste the working adults' beverage of choice.

"If you're thinking about going to that ditzy shop, fuhgeddaboudit!" the Mermaid said. "Not for nothing, but it is the absolute worst. Everyone made a huge deal about it when it first opened, but there's nothing there—no egg creams, no heros, no schmear, I mean, who serves a bagel without schmear?"

"So, then what do they have?" Dakota asked.

"Coffee, mostly, but don't expect to get a normal regular."

"But I want to try some."

"There's no use in getting coffee, yuppie," the Mermaid said. "Firstly, dollars to doughnuts you'll get addicted, your teeth will stain, and you'll become mad jittery. Secondly, the caffeine won't give you energy; why do you suppose people keep going back for it? And thirdly, that shop has no sense of cleanliness. Just look at all that coffee and bubblestone!" There was no questioning the last statement because the ground near the establishment was littered with coffee beans and bubble-shaped tops of cups—a constant trashing of the walking area.

Dakota likened the coffee craze to his addiction to caramel apples. "But then how am I to taste the coffee without getting addicted?"

"There is some purpose for coffee, I suppose," the Mermaid went on. "If you were to get in the habit of drinking it, or at the very least, tell everyone you had the habit of drinking it. Imagine for a second that you were mad addicted, then you'd always have a reason to break from work. That would be a dumb good excuse, something I should put in my sea shell for future use."

She kept her eyes closed while she spoke, and this Dakota thought was a sign of poor manners. "But I guess it would be best to keep her eyes like that," he thought, "to avoid the sun."

Then he addressed her again, seeking a solution and not another medicine. "How should I drink coffee without getting addicted?"

"Oh, I just love it here—it certainly beats the tar beach on top of the building where all those flying rats gather," the Mermaid replied rather carelessly. "I plan to lie here all day, working on my tan, for my skin is not quite right, being so white."

In the next moment a few roasted coffee beans skimmed across the ground, past the tops of cups, and came to a stop in the water that had been spilled near the fountain, but they didn't seem to bother the Mermaid one bit. "Or maybe half the day. I don't want to turn into a prune!"

"But how can I taste the coffee without being addicted?" Dakota asked a pitch louder, having not gotten the answer he had hoped for.

"Is it even possible to try coffee and not get mad addicted?" the Mermaid asked.

Dakota pondered this question and the people who consumed the hot refreshment for a moment. His dad drank it *every* morning. So did his teacher. "It doesn't seem like one can," he thought. "My goodness, why, drinking coffee is like smoking!"

"Maybe I will stay for a few hours; I don't want to get skin cancer."

"Should I not drink coffee at all?" Dakota asked.

"That is up to you. If you want to stand *on line* for that cockamamie coffee, go right ahead." The Mermaid flipped over to lie on her front. "Now, please, go see where you got to go. A good tan requires a little quiet time."

"Ugh, all she thinks about is her appearance," Dakota muttered to himself as he approached the shop, then stopped and gaped.

The coffeehouse was a giant glass tree; the trunk, the branches, and the leaves were all glass, and so were the roots and floor, which was the only glassy area in the courtyard. Glass ball ornaments, painted light shades of the color spectrum, had little messages on them, like "Depresso. The feeling you get when you've run out of coffee," and "A yawn is a silent scream for coffee."

In the trunk there was an open rectangular space with a Moose standing on its hind legs in the tree, wearing a coffee-colored apron, preparing the refreshment with its humanlike hands. A woman with a big, blonde wig that made her face look very small was drinking a beverage and stood outside the tree in a dull gray business dress—Dakota guessed she was the Bigwig. A shiny goldfish appeared in the counter, which was a fish tank filled with roasted coffee seeds for pebbles. A sign on the trunk above the Moose read, "Glass Tree Coffeehouse: A Taste of the Midwest," and it was of course made of glass with the letters colored a greenish hue. The whole place smelled of roasted beans.

"What a mighty coffee spill!" Dakota thought, as he crunched on the seeds and tops of cups that littered the glass floor. "You've all had too much coffee."

They certainly had had too much of it. The Bigwig trembled incessantly, and as for the goldfish, it sucked on the "pebbles" and vibrated constantly. The only things in the shop that did not shake were the Moose barista and a curious, little, coffee-bean-spotted dog, which hid behind the transparent tree, wagging its tail, and peeked at Dakota every minute or so.

Sameer Garach

"Can someone tell me why that dog keeps eating coffee beans?" Dakota asked in a tone of great worry in the general direction of the beings, unaware whom the dog belonged to.

"It's a Westchester Whelp," the Bigwig answered at once, "and it only likes to feel a buzz. Have some more, fish!"

She ordered the goldfish to taste the "pebbles" with such force that Dakota experienced a quick jolt of alertness, like that of a caffeine rush. But seeing that she did not mean to frighten him, he went on thinking of Bernie and the welfare of dogs in general, then remarked, "Dogs cannot have coffee." Before Dakota could add more to his warning, the Bigwig started up.

"Everyone knows a dog cannot have coffee," she said quite condescendingly. "What, you think you're so clever for figuring that one out? Don't pretend to be important. The Bigwig is important; only what the Bigwig says matters."

Dakota did not at all like her words nor her tone. And he had never heard anyone talk about himself or herself in the third person; it was rather silly and made him feel very distant from her. "Come, there's no use in feeling less than her and losing your temper. I should think everyone is important, not a few people," he muttered to himself. As this conversation was begging for more arguments, he made up his mind to change the subject. While he tried to fix a topic that would not give rise to quarrels, the Moose opened the fish tank and poured coffee seeds until it became half full of beans, which caused a great mess, as he displaced water from the tank and made the floor all wet.

"What are you doing?" Dakota asked, worried that the fish might get sick or die from coffee the way dogs do.

"This is a coffee shop, dontchaknow. I can't have it smell like fish!" the Moose said in a peculiar male accent.

"More coffee!" the Bigwig demanded.

Here the Moose poured a cup of coffee beans and added some sugar, then moved the cup past his head and poked a little hole in the bottom of it with his antler and started stirring the contents. Once he finished, he gave the leaking cup to the Bigwig.

"Is it hot?" she asked.

"You betcha," the Moose answered.

The Bigwig splashed the coffee beans on her face and exclaimed, "Refreshing!"

"Oh yah, would you like some more?"

65

"Why, certainly."

And the Moose showered her, and incidentally the floor, with coffee seeds by throwing cups full of beans at her. The strangest part was that the Bigwig stared wide-eyed through it all and looked like a zombie.

"She's incredibly stupid!" Dakota thought, thoroughly puzzled by her behavior. "Maybe she can't blink because she's too alert."

"Please stop making a mess. Someone could slip and fall!" Dakota cried, concerned for the safety of the customers, whenever they came, and himself.

"If everybody would stop complaining about work conditions—it's not safe here, there's not enough personal time, and so on—" the Bigwig said in a contemptuous tone, "the business would be more productive."

"But shouldn't a workplace be safe?" Dakota said, glad to have an opportunity to exercise his little wisdom. "People can't go walking around holding scissors. Otherwise, they might get hurt. And what's wrong with time for oneself? I don't think anyone can go on all day; the fire does go out, right?"

"Speaking of fire," the Bigwig said, "you should be fired! Nagging like you do."

Dakota glanced at the Moose, who slaved feverishly filling coffee cups with beans and seemed quite focused on the task at hand, so he continued. "Wouldn't working all the time make you tired?"

"Oh, please, what do you know?" she said in a contemptuous tone. "You're no one. Don't bother the Bigwig with hours. The Bigwig puts in more than anybody—she has the bandwidth to take on any project." Here she began taking one cup at a time from the line of cups and splashing herself with the roasted seeds.

"When I work too much, I get tired and mess up," poor Dakota muttered to himself.

Then she yelped, "The Bigwig is hungry," and without ordering and waiting for the Moose to fetch the goldfish and cook it, the Bigwig fished out the animal from the little aquarium with her bare hands and said, "Here fishy, fishy, fishy!" while the Moose shouted, "Uff da!" then repeatedly warned, "You fetch it, you bought it." She splashed water everywhere, as the goldfish was hard to catch, considering it shook so much, but at last the Bigwig caught the animal and put it on a bed of coffee beans in a basket lined with a little red-and-white checkered wrapper.

Suddenly, the Bigwig's watch beeped. "Oh, shoot! Where has the time gone?" Then she turned to Dakota and, handing him the basket, said, "Here! You can have it. The Bigwig has a golf match with the Big Boss." In another moment she was gone.

Dakota faced the Moose, who quickly said, "No returns!"

Confused the meal was not the familiar fish and chips he was accustomed to, Dakota asked, "Fish and coffee?"

"You betcha. Dontchaknow, it's in the blood of an American to do the opposite of the rest of the world," the Moose said. "Just look at our measurement system."

The goldfish tossed about the basket when Dakota received it, and he wondered whether it kept doing this because it was out of the water or because it had been gently biting the coffee beans. "Poor little fishy," he thought. "Am I supposed to eat this?" At first he reasoned he would set out by treating the animal like sushi, eating it with chopsticks, but on second thought, *that* was raw fish, and this was a live fish. The basket trembled in Dakota's hands more than before, as the fish doubled itself up rapidly, and he felt sorry for the fish. "Maybe I can save it by putting it in the fountain." As soon as he figured out the best way to handle the fish, he walked away from the shop and into the sitting area with the elephants. "If I leave it here," Dakota thought, "the coffee shop will let it die. Wouldn't that be terrible?"

Just then the goldfish stopped flipping, and Dakota looked at the animal very carefully to see that it was in fact dead. There was no mistaking the fish's end because it no longer moved and its skin began to dry. Soon its eyes disappeared and turned into depressions on either side of its face, and its mouth changed into a smile. The gold skin became crusty, and the fish hardened, baked under the sun, into a cracker. And Dakota thought, "Why, I have a goldfish cracker!" He looked closely at the fish to make sure it was in fact edible.

Yes, it seemed quite all right to eat. "But what if it really has gone stale?" Dakota thought about this a good deal before he munched on it because he'd never seen what had happened to a fish under the sun, and he was fairly certain that when you were served fish, it didn't turn into a cracker after being left out for so long. "Oh, I shouldn't want to eat something that has gone bad." He stared at the basket of food; it was determined long before that he wouldn't eat the coffee beans, but now the fish also looked out of the question, so he felt that it would be no use to carry the food any farther.

Dakota set the basket down on the fountain's edge and was glad that he didn't eat the food. "If I had eaten the fish and coffee," he said to himself, "I would have had a tummy ache." He started to think about the times he had eaten too many goldfish crackers and gotten a stomach ache. "If only I could control myself when it comes to goldfish—"

Suddenly, he became startled by something moving between his legs and looked down in a hurry. Relieved to see it was only the Westchester Whelp, he sighed.

The dog wagged its tail and smiled at Dakota, which made the animal appear friendly, except that it coughed up a coffee bean, so he thought it might be sick.

"Here, little girl," he said, noting the animal's anatomy as he crouched low to pet her. The dog wagged her tail more quickly. "What a nice doggy!" Then he asked, confident that she could talk, "Can you tell me how to get to the top of the tower?"

"That depends on how you want to get there," the Whelp replied, and it occurred to Dakota by the sound of her voice that she was the same dog who had urged him to enter the beehive earlier.

"It doesn't matter how I get there."

"There are two paths: one is fast and easy, the other, slow and difficult."

"Oh, it must be fast and easy," Dakota said in a great hurry. He was growing impatient with the creatures of the New World, for he longed to see the city from above and touch the clouds.

"That will certainly be the case," the Whelp said, "as long as you don't mind having the ends justify the means."

Of course Dakota had no doubts about this, so he asked, "How will I get there and what are the ends?"

"Over there—" the Whelp pointed with her snout to an exit different from the one Dakota had used to enter the courtyard "—there is a Ladder of Diminishing Rungs, or corporate ladder, you'll have to climb. It's a very dog-eat-dog type of ladder. It will lead you to a peculiar boardroom, where you'll meet a lion, or the Fiscal Feline, and an 800-pound Gorilla."

"Holy seeds!" Dakota said in a tone of alarm.

"There's no need to worry. They're both lifeless, zombie-like."

"But I don't want to go near zombies," Dakota cried, taking the zombie thing very literally and wondering what a lion-zombie and gorilla-zombie might look like.

"Oh, you can't avoid that. We're all lifeless here. I'm lifeless. You're lifeless."

"But I'm not a zombie. I'm not lifeless," Dakota protested.

"You are," the Whelp said as a matter of fact. "Otherwise, you wouldn't have gotten a job here."

At this Dakota became puzzled. But seeing that the dog kept wagging her tail, as though she longed for a game of fetch, he asked, "And how are you lifeless?"

"Now, a dog in itself is not lifeless. You agree?"

"I don't see how any dog is lifeless," Dakota said rather sharply. "But do go on."

"Well, I'm an old dog. And you can't teach an old dog new tricks. Do you agree?"

"Why, yes, my mom always used to tell me that."

"But do you know why?"

After Dakota gave it some thought, he said, "I haven't the slightest idea."

Here the Whelp cleared her throat and tried to explain herself. "Now, you agree a dog who's full of life can learn new tricks?"

"Well, yes," Dakota said quite sure.

"And a dog without a life can't?"

"Yes, that all sounds right to me."

"Therefore, I must be a lifeless dog if I can't learn new tricks."

Dakota looked away to the ground and rubbed his chin with a face of confusion before saying, "I would call it being stubborn."

"And you're as stubborn as a mule," the Whelp quipped.

Dakota was about to argue that he looked more like a stallion, and he had proof because the jenny had told him so, but remembered he had eaten some chips and was not as slender and elegant as he once was.

"Are you playing golf today with the Big Boss?" the Whelp asked before coughing up another coffee seed. "If you climb the Ladder of Diminishing Rungs, you're invited."

"I would like to, except I haven't any clubs," Dakota replied in a wishful tone.

"The clubs will be provided. All you have to do is show," the Whelp said in an encouraging tone.

And so the match was set. Dakota was not surprised in the least bit that clubs would be available, for he was quite accustomed to there always being whatever one needed in the New World. He bid farewell to the Whelp and began on his way, except the dog followed close behind and coughed.

"What happened to the goldfish?" the Whelp inquired in a concerned tone, as though they were friends.

"It dried and became the *cracker sort*," Dakota replied, observing a bean in front of the dog.

"Did you have coffee with your *Sacher torte*?"

"I said cracker," Dakota said calmly, then with an unpleasant temper about him, "Why do you keep eating and spitting coffee beans?"

"How else am I to work like a dog?" the Whelp said in an offended tone. "The world runs on coffee, you know."

Dakota furrowed his brows, puzzled as to what kind of work a dog did. At any rate he had little desire to stick around and waste more time, so he continued walking toward the Ladder of Diminishing Rungs. "I don't want to face zombies, especially not lion and gorilla types!" he muttered to himself. "Maybe I could get off at a different floor and not have to see them. Yes, that's what I'll do."

The dog coughed, and when Dakota turned to look at her, she was standing behind him with a roasted seed a short way off.

"I think you should stop having coffee. It's clearly not good for you," he said, delighted to be the adult in the conversation.

"It's terrible," the Whelp remarked. "People say that work kills them, but if everyone drinks coffee to work, maybe it's really coffee that kills."

"So, you intend to kill yourself then?"

"At this old age I'm better off dead than alive," the Whelp said rather morbidly, "you'll come to see it that way, too."

"Well, I would hope not," Dakota said, annoyed by her talk of growing old and dying. "Now shoo. Be gone, go on now, shoo."

The dog moaned, then turned away and followed the trail of roasted seeds she had coughed up on her way to Dakota.

"Well, I've never seen a dog eat and spit out coffee beans," Dakota thought, "nor a dog that works! I will have to tell Bernie this whenever I get back."

Sameer Garach

Soon he found an extraordinary sculpture, a pile of people—all wearing dull gray masks—stuck in their place and stacked upon each other in the shape of a pyramid. Dakota wondered where the Ladder of Diminishing Rungs was and turned around to see if the Westchester Whelp had followed him so that he could ask her for directions. The dog watched him from afar and shouted, "That's it! Hurry, you'll be late!" Dakota faced the "Ladder of Diminishing Rungs," and his gaze followed it up to the next floor, where it seemed to end, with no other levels in between for him to exit.

"How am I ever going to get up this ladder?" Average-sized Dakota would have to step over stone people to get to the top.

"If you have trouble advancing," the dog yelled, "just remember this learning: who you know is far more important than what you know."

He nodded slowly, wondering who could help him, and stuck his foot in the air rather timidly all the while saying, "These people look awfully real. I wish it wasn't like this; I wish I had taken the slow and difficult way." His foot came down on an old lady with glasses, or she appeared that way given her mask.

"Ouch. Stop micromanaging me!" she complained.

Dakota blinked a few times, unsure whether he should proceed. The woman was made of rock yet could talk, and she seemed to be in pain. "Oh, I'm sorry, but in any case I don't think I can help you," he said in a subdued tone. It occurred to him that if he climbed quickly, there might be less suffering, inasmuch as a sculpture could feel.

He looked up and suddenly became surprised; the pile of stone people had some familiar faces—his coach, teacher, principal, and so on. Moreover, each recognizable figure had one of their hands turned out so that Dakota could grab onto it to pull himself up. In another moment it was decided that he would use the helping hands in this way and step on the foreigners. He took another step, this time on a young man.

"You don't listen!" Frustration was set in the man's mask.

Another step. "I can't meet that deadline. I've already got too much on my plate."

With every step, a new complaint honked, as though he were stepping on horns. Halfway up, he stopped to catch his breath and looked over his shoulder to see his progress. "Why, it's a long way down from up here. I hope I don't fall. It would really hurt." After a minute or two, he regained his breath to climb farther.

One after another, the voices continued their complaints: "I'm not disorganized. *You're* disorganized—Follow through on your promises—I'm getting nowhere. Why didn't I get the promotion?—How in the world did you get this job?—It's unfair pay!—Can't question your opinion—Thanks for the feedback. I could sure use it." This final one sounded sarcastic.

At last he reached the top of the Ladder of Diminishing Rungs and looked down from the floor he stood on; luckily, he knew enough people to help him get there. Within half a minute or so, the stone pyramid of people rumbled and collapsed, and dust filled the air. "Holy seeds, how will they ever rebuild?" Dakota said to himself in a tone of worry. "It sure takes a lot to get to the top, and only a few seconds for everything to crumble."

Chapter 8: A Vain Meeting

Dakota walked rather timidly down a hallway lit by wall-mounted torches; with each step, he felt less and less confident that he would find his way to an observation deck that would let him touch the clouds and see the city from above. There were many doors opposite one another, but only one was open, as the sound of waves crashing upon the shore invited him to go near it. When he looked through the doorway, he saw a cove with a sea green bay. On the beach, under the shade of the cliff, there was a large tree trunk split in half down its length that served as a table, with several stumps for chairs set out under a lamp—a jar filled with fireflies that hung from the rock ceiling by a vine—and a wooden boat turned upside down that formed a sort of counter to the side.

The 800-pound Gorilla and the Fiscal Feline, neither of which looked like zombies as Dakota had imagined, were having snacks at the split tree trunk; the lion had on a top hat and bow tie, and the two animals wore dull gray suit jackets, except the Gorilla's clothes were ripped in several places, unable to contain its massive size. A Cuckoo Bird sat opposite the lion in a dull gray sleeveless dress, bobbing its head, recording something on a stack of papers, so focused it hadn't noticed Dakota standing in the doorway, and the other two rested their heads in their hands, bored and nearly asleep, as they watched what the Cuckoo Bird was writing with weary eyes. "Must be very important," Dakota thought. "Maybe I should leave them be."

The Gorilla sat at the head of the table, and when Dakota started to move past the doorway, seeing that they might be too busy to be disturbed, the ape glanced at him with one eye and said, "Hurry! You're late!"

"I tried to get here as fast as possible!" Dakota cried, very confused about the time, and he sat on a stump near the child-sized Cuckoo Bird, as it appeared the least intimidating.

"Don't bother to help yourself," the 800-pound Gorilla said in an unwelcoming tone.

Dakota's eyes fell upon their food; the cubes of cheese had mold on them, the fruits were discolored and wrinkled, the bread was covered with white fuzz, and all of it had flies buzzing around.

"I'm sorry; in any case I don't see how I could."

"The hearty fare is for show only," the Gorilla said.

"Then it's not good of you to waste food," Dakota remarked angrily.

"And it's not good of you to waste our time!" the Gorilla rejoined in an offended tone.

"And without apologizing," the Fiscal Feline muttered, his gaze set on the papers.

"Consider this experience a learning: showing up is half the battle," the Cuckoo Bird said as she continued to write.

"I didn't know I was late," Dakota said rather innocently. "I was caught up—" Just then he checked himself before he began to blame the Westchester Whelp for the lengthy conversation he'd been dragged into, as he'd learned from the Blame Game that passing blame didn't solve anything.

At last the Fiscal Feline looked up from the papers in front of the Cuckoo Bird. "A review of the facts will show that we did not engage in misconduct. Mistakes were made. I deeply regret our current state of waste, and the waste generated by every event held by the Creature Company," he stated proudly, then added in a more personal tone, "Does that sound good enough to you?"

Dakota gaped, quite surprised by the great apology. "I think you should say sorry only if you mean it."

The Fiscal Feline stared at Dakota for a moment with a bewildered look of disappointment, then began, "The agenda for today's meeting: how can we achieve growth?" He looked at the Gorilla and dipped his head down as if to bow. "Think outside the box; creativity is appreciated."

Dakota found their kind behavior funny but held in his shriek of laughter as everyone looked very serious. "Why, I know how these animals can grow," he thought, then aloud with great delight, "I know how you can be taller."

The animals glanced at one another, then ignored the newcomer altogether. The Fiscal Feline turned to the Gorilla and was about to say something, opening his mouth, but after a moment, he said nothing and closed his jaw.

Here Dakota found an excellent opportunity to express his opinion, so he took the liberty to say, "Milk can help you grow; it does a body good."

The animals remained quiet for some time while Dakota waited for their approval. At last the Gorilla broke the silence and remarked to the Fiscal Feline, "That's expected from a newbie."

"We're talking about our trees," the Fiscal Feline clarified, facing Dakota.

"I know about trees. I've planted many in my backyard with my mom," Dakota said, eager to be of good help and show off his little knowledge. "If you use a good fertilizer with a lot of nutrients and water your trees daily, they'll grow fast."

"Money trees! Our investments!" the Fiscal Feline screamed with passion. "Coming up with random ideas is not the same as finding solutions! You don't understand the agenda."

"Oh, but—but you didn't say the directions," Dakota said rather wisely. The Gorilla and Fiscal Feline looked at each other and shook their heads in despair while Dakota added, "If you had been clear from the start, then all I know is if you want to grow something, you have to nourish it."

"How could we possibly use this?" the Gorilla cried, too upset to hear Dakota's last statement. "We need the best and right solution, not any solution. You do not value creativity."

"I absolutely value it," Dakota argued.

"And you tolerate uncertainty," the Cuckoo Bird chimed in, her head facing the papers on which she continued to write. "The risk is too high, like attempting to fly without having well-trained wings—I tell that to my boys all the time—and it comes from *you* not knowing what you're doing."

"There is a lack of concern for being right on your part," the Fiscal Feline said to Dakota and arrested the conversation.

The attendees to the meeting sat in silence for a minute or two and returned to looking bored, except for the Cuckoo Bird, which Dakota noticed was making tick marks in sets of five as she bobbed her head and counted. In the meantime poor Dakota felt left out and bad for speaking up, like he'd done something wrong, because his input was not prized the way it should be, as it was in school. And he began to see why this place was lifeless. "I should raise my hand and wait to be called on. That would be polite," he thought. In another moment he shut himself up like a telescope and resolved not to state his opinion so eagerly.

At last the Fiscal Feline spoke up and the meeting resumed. "Another thing we need to consider is raising capital." He took a small box out from his mane and pulled out a petty amount of cash from the box, then stared at the money for a moment, trying to read the value. The Fiscal Feline pulled at the currency's ends and pressed his humanlike paw on the bill on the tree trunk table to straighten out the wrinkles, and asked the Gorilla, "What is the cost of money?"

The Gorilla weighed this for some time, and Dakota kept mum and fidgeted on the stump, itching to participate.

When it became obvious that the Gorilla had no solution, the Fiscal Feline's eyes fell upon average-sized Dakota. "A penny for your thoughts."

"Money has no cost," Dakota said hastily without careful thought.

"The cost to make it!" the Fiscal Feline shot back, then turning to the 800-pound Gorilla with a growl, "I hate to say I told you so, but the green pen didn't work."

"The ink was low," the Gorilla said in a weak voice.

"Well, the bill's all smudgy now," the Fiscal Feline complained. "You shouldn't have tried to get ink out of the pen by going back and forth with it on the money."

"And you shouldn't have played the numbers game!" the Gorilla grunted. He snatched the bill and looked at it sadly, then grabbed the ink and a backup feather pen next to the Cuckoo Bird and dipped the pen into the black ink and tried to fix the smudge, which only made it worse. "A good green pen that it was."

Dakota had leaned over and viewed the money with raised brows. "Funny money! It has decimals, and not whole numbers!"

"There's nothing funny about money," the Fiscal Feline said with all seriousness. "Mine is just as reasonable as yours. Don't you change your money the way you see fit?"

"No, that would be counterfeit!" Dakota said, glad to show off his good behavior. Just then his reasons not to speak began to disappear. "And I should think that could land *you* in jail."

"But when you change the value, you can pay your way *out* of jail," the Fiscal Feline said rather haughtily.

Here Dakota felt at odds with the Fiscal Feline. His remark suggested that he might be up to some bad business, and yet he seemed very open about it. Then as nice as Dakota could manage, he said, "I'm not sure I trust you."

"Am I too money-minded?" the lion asked.

"You're absolutely greedy," Dakota said.

"All the richest people are." The Fiscal Feline grinned. "You don't have a whistle on you, do you?" the lion asked with beady eyes. And the Bird and Gorilla stared at Dakota in all seriousness.

"No, it's at home."

"Good. Keep it there. We don't appreciate whistleblowers," the Fiscal Feline said in a sharp tone, then returned his eyes to their normal size and turned away. "The Cuckoo Bird needs more paper!" he shrieked and jumped off his stump in a great hurry. He took a large cheese slicer and shaved a few thin pieces of wood from the upside-down boat and put them next to the Cuckoo Bird.

The Cuckoo Bird screamed, "The ink! Please someone, the ink!" And the 800-pound Gorilla hurled the colored fluid in her direction, and it would have smashed into her face and made a nasty mess, except the Fiscal Feline caught the ink before that happened and quickly put it down next to the Bird, then tended to his little humanlike paw, as it seemed to hurt.

"Have you figured out how to achieve growth yet?" the Fiscal Feline said to Dakota after his paw recovered.

"I'm afraid I haven't," Dakota replied in a meek voice, unsure of what to say after all his efforts had been ignored.

"There really is no such thing as growth, you know," the Fiscal Feline said. "But we invest a lot in research and development to have everyone believe that it exists. You see, change is inevitable, so when it arrives, it's important that we have a competitive advantage—like using the words *growth* and *advancement*, *progress* and *improvement*."

"I love progress," the Gorilla said with a great smile. "That's my favorite word."

"Mine is synergy," the Cuckoo Bird remarked. "I just love the way it sizzles on the tongue. Synergy."

"Now that's money well spent!" the Fiscal Feline continued. "But that's a trade secret, so don't tell anyone!"

"So, you want to have everyone believe you are better than them?" Dakota asked innocently, and the animals nodded. "Applesauce! I don't see how that's an advancement," he muttered, quite unimpressed. His posture drooped, and he sighed while staring at the table. "They're incredibly stupid! Anyway, I think business is not the subject for me," he thought, then aloud in a severe tone, "You should use your money more wisely than wasting it on coming up with ways to make yourself sound important."

"If you knew Money, you wouldn't have said that we are wasting him," the Fiscal Feline said in an offended tone. "For one, he doesn't exist anymore. What is left of him is a ghost, an illusion now. That's why everyone says, 'Money is an illusion.' You would know that if you were not so new."

"I'm afraid I don't know what you mean." Dakota felt this conversation was about to take a turn for the worse.

"I'm not surprised that you don't," the Fiscal Feline said rather haughtily. "Money is dead and gone, and I'm sure you didn't know him."

"I do too know about money," Dakota said in a furious passion. "Because whenever I find some, I save it in my piggy bank."

"You couldn't have saved Money," the Fiscal Feline growled. "How many times do I have to say it? Now if you had kept a close friendship with him, known Money, he'd change the value of your currency to pretty much whatever you liked, and you'd be able to buy almost anything. Suppose there was a big house you wanted, just what the American Dream is all about, you'd only have to tell him, and just like that, you would have a brand-new house!"

"If only it were that easy," the 800-pound Gorilla muttered. In another moment he slammed his fists on the table and yelled, "Why isn't it so?" A crack grew down the middle of the tree trunk, which Dakota believed was sure to end the meeting, but the Bird remained focused on the "papers," and the lion only glanced at the ape, then

78

stared at a bunch of tree trunk tables off to the side which had been split in half and ruined.

At first Dakota thought it was very rude of the Gorilla to lose his temper, but being that it seemed quite normal to go through tables, he returned to the conversation at hand. "Holy seeds, that would indeed be wonderful; one way, not to have to work for anything, and another way, to have everything!"

"Yes, you may feel like that in the beginning," the Fiscal Feline said, "but just think, you wouldn't learn much."

"Oh, but why not?" Dakota asked.

"Well, if it wasn't for work, I would never have learned about Money," the Fiscal Feline replied. "You see, Money was quite famous in his time. So the only way I could know him was to build my network. And even then, I had to work my tail off to really get to know him. Now I can look back and say I knew him, like *knew him knew him*; I had the benefit of a special relationship. I got him things, and he got me things. But as is the case with everyone around here, he turned lifeless, literally. It happened when we met last Christmas at the company holiday party—you know, the one held at the Big Boss's office—and my name was called for karaoke, to which the song that came up and I danced to was

'You put your money in,
You pull your money out;
You put your money in,
And you shake it all about.'

Have you heard of that song?"

"It sounds a bit like 'Hokcy Pokcy,'" Dakota replied.

"I've never heard of that," the Fiscal Feline said, "but the karaoke song goes like this:

'Everybody form an investment account.
You put your money in,
You pull your money out;
You put your money in,
And you shake it all about.
You do the choke-y broke-y,
And your life turns upside down.

Dakota and the American Dream

That's what it's all about!

> You put your savings in,
> You pull your savings out;
> You put your savings in,
> And you shake it all about.
> You do the choke-y broke-y,
> And your life turns upside down.
> That's what it's all about!'"

The Cuckoo Bird joined in the festive mood while recording the tick marks, "You put your head in, you pull your hair out; you put your head in, and you pull your hair all out—" and continued until the Fiscal Feline and Gorilla both shouted, "Pay attention to the minutes!" And Dakota gathered the Cuckoo Bird might be recording time.

"What's a choke-y broke-y?" Dakota put to all three of them.

"It's when someone chokes—makes a poor investment decision—and goes broke—loses most or all of their money," the Fiscal Feline answered. "Anyway, I never got through the whole thing," he said in a melancholy tone, "and that's because I tripped and knocked over the money tree—you know, the tree on which Money lived and grew up in—into the office fireplace. And the Big Boss yelled, 'The money tree's burning!' and to me a few moments later, 'You're fired!'"

"That's terrible!" Dakota said.

"I was never really fired—the Big Boss had only lost his temper, you know—but since the tree's death," the Fiscal Feline went on as gloomy as before, "the business has no cash flow. And because Money was destroyed, Time was, too, because Time is Money. So you see, the Cuckoo Bird here has to record the minutes, for if she didn't, we wouldn't know the hour!"

"Holy seeds," Dakota said in a voice of wonder, "this is all so . . . interesting"—then seeing the dirty looks he got, he quickly recovered himself with—"I mean very sad."

"Yes, and because Money was so famous, he couldn't do what the average person could; so he was always limited. In addition to being called Time, Money became known as a Constraint. Now that Money is gone, there is no Constraint. So the Gorilla—he was once 400 pounds—can't stop eating. He's free to eat whatever and whenever he

80

wants! That's just one example. It used to be that only those who knew Money could have financial freedom. Now everyone's free."

Dakota nodded, as it all started to make sense. "Is that why at your meetings you are free to do whatever you like?"

"Yes, because Money has been destroyed," the Fiscal Feline said, "there is no Constraint on what we do."

"Then meetings are utterly useless, a big waste of time?" Dakota pointed out.

"We're not talking about this matter going forward," the 800-pound Gorilla said in such a decided tone that no one dared to argue with him. "It's depressing and bores me to death. Why don't you tell us what you did over the weekend, young man?"

"Oh, I, well I, I worked in my backyard." Dakota scowled, upset that he couldn't come up with anything more exciting to match the lion's story.

The Fiscal Feline yawned, and the Gorilla turned to the Cuckoo Bird, rather gloomy, and asked, "How about you? How was your weekend?"

"Yes, please share," Dakota said at once, eager to know how these animals spent their lives away from the "office."

"Only the details, mind you," the Fiscal Feline warned the Cuckoo Bird, "so you are not distracted from work."

"I know that; you don't have to keep reminding me," the Cuckoo Bird said in an annoyed tone. She smacked her lips, and Dakota wondered whether the Bird was stalling just for the sake of stalling. "I met two birds, different kinds, stuck in a tree," she began all the while recording the minutes, "away from my black forest home. One went by Jack—he was a donkey with wings—and the other, Pheasant."

"Why were they stuck?" Dakota asked, curious to know why they didn't just fly away.

"They were stuck because of the gum," the Cuckoo Bird replied.

Here Dakota imagined stepping into gum on the sidewalk and getting stuck in it. "That must indeed be a big, sticky piece of gum," he thought.

Next, he noticed the Cuckoo Bird, as well as the other creatures, wore shoes, so he asked, "Couldn't they have taken their shoes off?"

"Who wears shoes when they're at home?" the Cuckoo Bird put to the group.

"Not I," the Fiscal Feline said, then the Gorilla followed with, "Me neither."

"I don't either," Dakota remarked at once, a little embarrassed he'd asked the question in the first place (for, you see, after a moment or two it occurred to him that trees were homes to birds).

"Don't interrupt her with silly questions going forward," the Fiscal Feline said in a severe tone. "She can't be distracted to tend to your every fancy."

"I won't ask such a question again," Dakota recovered, his cheeks a little red, then to the Cuckoo Bird, "Please go on."

"As I was saying," the Cuckoo Bird chirped loudly, then softened her tone and said, "these two birds found food hard to come by." She paused and bobbed her head up and down as she counted the tick marks.

Dakota sighed but urged the Bird to continue. "Then what did they eat?"

"Gum," the Cuckoo Bird said at last. "That's all there was. Gumballs everywhere."

"I need more food," the Fiscal Feline interrupted in a shrill voice. "Hold on while I get some." He tiptoed on his hind legs to the upside-down boat that served as a counter—unlike the normal grace and confidence you see lions exhibit—and retrieved more of the spoiled food. He sat on his stump and licked his lips, ready to feast. The inedible gave off an acidic, vomit-like odor, and Dakota swallowed, disgusted. "Go on."

"Wait! I'm hungry also," the Gorilla screamed. While he plodded to the counter and snatched whatever food was left, the Fiscal Feline threw the old food, the food there before he got up, into the trash can. The Gorilla returned and sat down with such force, the stump buckled under his weight, the sand formed a mound beneath the table and made it rise a few inches, and the jar filled with fireflies swung from side to side. "Now go on."

In the meantime Dakota rubbed his chin, thinking where the story was heading. He couldn't see a lesson in it and wondered if the Bird really was cuckoo, so he asked with a tone of confusion, "How can a tree have gumballs? They would roll right off, wouldn't they?"

"It must have been a sweet gum tree," the Fiscal Feline figured, "so it's only natural that it would have gumballs in it."

"Yes," the Cuckoo Bird said. "So, you see it was quite a sticky situation." She dipped her feather pen in the ink quickly, so as to not lose time, and continued making tick marks on the "paper" before starting up again. "Now the Pheasant keeps taking orders from the Jackbird, because orders always come from above, and flaps his wings as he's told, with the hope that he might soar to the Jack's level, but the Jackbird just pats him on the back with a twig for giving it his best. But either way, they're both stuck in the hierarchy."

"What hierarchy is this you speak of?" Dakota asked.

"The corporate hierarchy," the Fiscal Feline answered.

Dakota scratched his head for a moment or two, then said very politely, "I'm sorry, I'm afraid I don't know what you mean." The Fiscal Feline and Gorilla looked at him. "I hope you are not offended, but your story makes no sense. Please don't be offended. I'm sorry."

The Cuckoo Bird looked up from her tick marks and stared at the new guy.

"The minutes!" the Fiscal Feline growled, and the Cuckoo Bird returned to the "paper."

"I'm sorry to distract you," Dakota said to the Bird. "It's not helping you finish."

"Tsk, tsk. Now who's making fake apologies?" the Fiscal Feline quipped.

Dakota was surprised, as he found himself doing things he had warned others not to do, and made up his mind not to say much.

The Cuckoo Bird switched to a new piece of "paper" and continued as before. "Jack sits on a higher branch than Pheasant and poops on him. When the top-level Jack looks down, he only sees poop, and when the low-level Pheasant looks up, he sees an Ass. They are stuck, so that is the hierarchy now, and neither can change it. Choice has made it clear that they never had it, and anyone like the Pheasant can't stand to bear it."

"Neither can I!" average-sized Dakota screamed with passion. He couldn't stay silent, for the story was not quite what he wanted to hear. "That's not fair! I can indeed be what I want to be. And—and the posters on the wall at school say I can achieve my dreams."

"Posters?" the Gorilla scoffed. "I wanted to be a lean, mean, chest-pounding machine. Now I weigh 800 pounds and can't fit into my clothes."

Dakota observed his ripped suit jacket and thought, "Poor animal."

"Do you suppose I desired to live in a poor black forest?" the Cuckoo Bird asked. "A wealthy white forest would be much better." Then her voice turned into a nagging one. "But no, I have to keep up this endless routine of recording minutes."

"Do you believe I fancy being a financial nerd?" the Fiscal Feline said. "I never had the courage to be promoted to the King of the Jungle—it's always the Fiscal Feline—so now I'm stuck where I am, in this wretched hierarchy. But there's a useful learning to be gained through all of this: Not everyone's cut out for a management position. Not everyone's meant to get to the *top*. Some are content with it, others aren't."

This nugget of truth was more than average-sized Dakota could take at the moment; he stood and stormed out the peculiar boardroom, or cove, at once. "I want to go to the *top*, touch the clouds and see the city," he whined. In another minute he stopped and thought it was rude of him to lose his temper and walk away, so he returned, half hoping they would understand his nature and half afraid they wouldn't. The Cuckoo Bird continued recording the minutes while the other two peered over her shoulder and watched.

"Don't forget to mark through that set of four," the Fiscal Feline reminded.

"I won't!" the Cuckoo Bird said in an offended tone and flapped both her wings as to dismiss the large cat. "I know what I'm doing, mind you."

"How many minutes is that?" the Gorilla put to the Bird.

"Why haven't any of you come after me?" Dakota asked rather timidly, afraid that he might interrupt the work and be scolded.

"You can go," the Fiscal Feline said with a steely glare, just before he picked up the large cheese slicer and started to make more "paper" from the wooden boat. "You're only here at your own will."

At this Dakota turned away and left them for good. "I don't think they want me, so why should I stay? I should go where I am wanted," he thought. Just then he shut himself up like a telescope and, instead of returning to the hallway of doors, started climbing a staircase carved into the rock amid the sound of waves, hoping to find new friends with better lessons to learn. "I had never been to a meeting until now, but I dare say it's the most useless thing there ever was!"

In another minute he made his way up the steps and met a pit of rising sand. "That's curious," he said to himself, "but everything in the

New World is. I don't see why I shouldn't go any farther." So average-sized Dakota began to mount the sloping sand and when he looked over the horizon, to his great delight there was a golf course.

"Holy seeds! Now if I can just figure out where that golf match starts, I'll be having fun in no time!" He weaved through some tall grass and found himself walking alone on the fairway. Soon he came to the end of it and mounted a hill.

Dakota and the American Dream

Chapter 9: The Big Boss's Golf Course

A large, nearly round putting green stood at the top of the hill, surrounded by bunkers and with a lake behind it, and there were three birds squatting. The birds on the green were of different sizes—small, medium, and large—and they were busy laying eggs all around the green at varying distances from the hole—close, closer, and closest. Dakota found this whole matter very interesting, so he tiptoed a few feet closer—he didn't want to scare them—to get a better view, then heard the smallest bird chirp in a little voice, "Eagle, don't lay your egg so close to the hole!"

"Birdie, it has to be easy to make!" the Eagle said in a sharp tone. "Albatross is laying her egg even closer!"

"I have to live up to my name," the Albatross said in an offended voice. "It's not my fault you're an Eagle."

"Oh hush!" the Eagle cried. "At least I'm not afraid to be fired!"

Then the Birdie mocked, "Albatross toadies up to the Big Boss! Albatross toadies up to the Big Boss!"

"I do not!" the Albatross squawked angrily. "I'm what you call a professional."

"A professional toady!" the Eagle ridiculed. "That's why the Big Boss always wins."

Albatross stood, her egg halfway out, and snapped, "Be a team player! Deals are sealed on the green!" She happened to see Dakota looking at her and told the others, "Shh, here comes one," to which all of them sprang up—they finished laying their eggs with looks of constipation on their faces—and pretended to walk about as though they were just ordinary birds on the green.

"Can any of you tell me," Dakota began, "why you are laying eggs on the green?"

The Eagle and Albatross kept their beaks sealed, but as for the Birdie, she started to sweat in fear and said in a meek voice, "Well, you see, we are greenskeepers, and—" The Eagle and Albatross looked severely at the little bird with big eyes and shook their heads in disapproval. "—oh, nothing." The Birdie smiled nervously.

"Out with it," Dakota demanded, crowding around the small bird. "Come on. You can't hide what you did."

The Birdie's eyes turned to the Eagle, then the Albatross, both of whom were looking as stern as before. Dakota edged closer, and the Birdie crouched down in fear in his great shadow. "Why, what had happened was that we interfered with the golf balls while they were in the air"—she looked at the other birds, who sighed and rolled their eyes—"I mean it was an accident. So we are fixing our mistake before the Big Boss's company arrives, because if he finds that his ball is not in a favorable spot, we'll all be fired!"

In the next moment the Eagle, who kept an eagle eye on the fairway, squawked, "The Big Boss! The Big Boss!" and the three birds started walking about and looking for worms in the grass, plucking every so often, which seemed rather awkward for the Eagle and Albatross, as they tried to mimic the Birdie. Suddenly, a chorus of voices and a clattering of golf clubs came from down the fairway, and average-sized Dakota stood on his tippy toes and looked over the edge of the hill, anxious to see the Big Boss and his company.

In front were the employees: the Drone and a herd of people with masks on. It was fairly obvious that they were guests and not players as they all wore shirts with a single question mark followed by the letter *t*.

Next came the caddies and players. The caddies, carrying clubs in sacks with dental floss straps and rubbing their necks all the while, looked about the sky as if they had never seen it before. They were an odd bunch: four old turtles—clearly lifers and all wearing bibs— walked on their hind legs slightly ahead of whoever they caddied for.

Among this group, the recognizable Greenback Squirrel kept listening and nodding to everything the players said, and as the procession came nearer, Dakota could hear him saying, "Ayuh, I ordered everything off the menu—subs, egg rolls, frankfurts, tonic, frappes, hoodsies with the jimmies, you name it. The country club will have the food all set by the time we finish."

At the end of the procession was a foursome of players: the Chairman, a man with a chair glued to his behind and a glowing brown nose, the Chief, a Native American tribal leader, the Big Cheese, a giant block of cheese, and the Big Boss, a man with a giant, orange head, whiskery eyebrows, and a golden fox for hair. They were all wearing dull gray suits and red ties, except the fox of course.

The Big Boss had no facial hair, and his eyes, oh his eyes, were as cold and blue as an iceberg. His whole face in fact was so serious and callous that it made Dakota shiver. It was as though the man had never smiled. His face bore wrinkles and carried a most disagreeable frown, as though he liked nothing and could never like anything. And oh, how shrewd he looked. How grim and severe and devoid of life.

Here Dakota considered whether he should hide behind the trees and not come in the way of the game, like the three greenskeepers seemed to be doing. "But the Westchester Whelp said I could play," he thought, "so long as I climbed the Ladder of Diminishing Rungs, and they would have clubs for me." So Dakota waited on the green for the procession.

When the crew made it uphill, the Drone waved at Dakota—he gestured similarly, pleased to see his interviewer—and the guests went around the green and cleared a way for the participants. In another minute the players and caddies came to a halt and looked at Dakota, and the Big Boss shouted with passion, "Move out of the way, greenskeeper!"

The Big Boss seemed very intimidating to average-sized Dakota, what with his big head and deep voice. Dakota stared blankly at the group, and while he thought how he should manage, the Big Boss ordered, "State your name, young man."

"My name is Dakota," he said in a trembling voice. "I climbed the Ladder of Diminishing Rungs."

"I'll judge how far you get," the Big Boss declared. "How'd he—" the Big Boss muttered to himself, keeping his eyes on Dakota, then with thunder, "How'd you get here before us?"

"I used a shortcut," wise Dakota ventured to say, then he pointed and added, "Over there is a staircase."

"What, you think you're better than us?" the Big Boss retorted, then talked under his breath. "And what are you doing with those balls?" He was referring to the eggs the three birds had laid moments ago.

"Nothing," Dakota said, then daringly added, to play along, "except looking for my ball!"

"The nerve of him!" the Big Boss rejoined to the Chairman, then to Dakota, "It is somewhere in the rough, or in one of them hazards, not on the green!" He mumbled something Dakota couldn't catch and turned red with fury before yelling, "You're fired!"

"Who died and made you boss?" Dakota shot back with courage that surprised himself. "I don't work for you."

"That's what makes this troublesome," the Big Boss lamented. "Somebody find who hired this fool and tell him to fire this man!"

The Chairman's brown nose glowed, then he leaned over to the Big Boss and said, "Please don't boss him around, my superior; he is only a greenskeeper!"

The Big Boss turned to the three birds and with anger in his voice yelled, "Move those birds!"—then in a softer tone—"We have a game to play."

Here Dakota became worried about the fate of the birds, for the Big Boss had made a poor first impression.

While the Squirrel was busy pointing to the caddies and ordering, "You heard the Big Boss, get rid of those birds!" the Big Boss winked at the birds, and the birds nodded. Moreover, the Chairman flashed a sly smile.

As the caddies—the turtles—started after the birds, the Birdie muttered, "Have to make the Big Boss look good," and the Eagle grumbled, "Got to love company politics!" And it occurred to wise Dakota that the whole thing had been planned. The Birdie first tried one of the bunkers but seeing that an alligator was in it, ran deep into the rough, where the grass was very high. The Eagle soared high up into a tree, and the Albatross jumped into the lake and swam away.

"Leave them alone!" Dakota shrieked.

The caddies chased the birds to the edge of their respective hazards, then quietly returned to the game.

"Are they far enough to not interfere?" the Big Boss asked.

"Very far, sir," the caddies said all at once.

"Showed them who's boss!" the Big Boss remarked in a witty manner, then standing over the Albatross's egg, which was right next to the golf hole, "This putt is a given. Mark it on the scorecard that I needed only two strokes on this par five."

"Ayuh, sir," the Squirrel said, as it fumbled with the pencil and scorecard. "Wicked excellent game you are having!"

"As usual." The Big Boss yawned and adjusted his hair—the fox on his head—as the Squirrel held up a hand mirror, then faced Dakota and asked, "Can you play golf?"

"Yes, I play it with my dad," Dakota replied eagerly.

"Very well. We will start a new round. To the next hole!" the Big Boss announced, and in another moment the crew picked up their "golf balls" and started to walk again.

At first Dakota smiled, glad to begin the game. However, a short time later he uttered in a timid and concerned voice, "Will you break the eggs?" But the Big Boss failed to acknowledge him, and Dakota joined and wondered what would happen next, especially because the game was fixed for the Big Boss.

"What up, kid?" The Greenback Squirrel had sneaked up and startled him. "It's a wicked good day for golf. Much better than that nor'easter we had last week."

"Oh, yes, the wind is low and the sun is behind the clouds," Dakota remarked (for, you see, he had spent some time with his father on the golf course and learned about good playing conditions and such things). "Where's the Bigwig? She said she'd be here."

"Shh!" the Squirrel shushed at once, one claw over his mouth. He took Dakota by the arm and pulled him to a water cooler off to the side for a quiet discussion. "She's left work—a temporary leave of absence—because she's under investigation, and if you ask me, she'll probably be fired."

"For what?"

The Squirrel took a cup and began to fill it with water. "Rumor has it that she's romantically involved with the old tookie, the Big Boss," he whispered.

Here Dakota giggled and thought, "Boss and the Wig, sitting in a tree, K-I-S-S-I-N-G," which was interrupted by the Squirrel.

"Don't tell anyone that I told you." He chugged down the water and commented, "Tastes like it came from a bubbler," then returned to the conversation. "Last I heard, she was the one who made the advance, and the Big Boss went—"

"It's tee time!" the Big Boss yelled to start the new round of golf. The players and caddies lined up in a hurry, and the caddies pulled out little frogs from their pockets and placed them on the ground. The frogs began hopping away; however, they settled down in a short time, as the caddies ordered them to do tee tricks, in which they were to stand on their hind legs and act like golf tees.

Dakota never had seen such a bizarre golf match, and he wondered how their clubs would manage to hit the eggs without hurting the little frogs. But once the eggs were placed on the "tees," which happened with some difficulty, as the frogs struggled to hold up the heavy eggs, the clubs were drawn from the sacks by the players. However, the clubs were not ordinary—metal or wood—the way you might think, but live snakes.

The Greenback Squirrel handed Dakota a snake from a golf bag, and when average-sized Dakota mustered enough courage to hold it, the most challenging part he found was getting it to stay straight. The slipperiness of the snake's skin did not at all help, as Dakota's hands kept sliding off the snake, and he nearly gave up until the Greenback Squirrel gave him a pair of gloves to wear so he could get a good grip on it. Just when he had straightened the reptile out, the egg he placed on the frog kept falling off and rolling away. And it occurred to Dakota that golf was much harder than it looked and required a great deal of patience.

When the time came to tee off, none of the players waited for the others, and they all swung at once. The snakes swallowed the eggs on the downswing, and the players put one hand above their eyes to form a visor and squinted as they looked for their egg balls in the sky. In the next moment a fight broke out among the players because some of them had let their snakes fly and without yelling *fore*. The Big Boss's orange head turned crimson with fury, and he blew steam—real steam came out from his mouth, ears, and nose—at those players who hit errant shots without shouting *fore*.

He pointed to a player and screamed, "You're fired!" then to another player, "You're fired!" In another moment the competitors collapsed as though struck by lightning. And the Big Boss kept going like this until he had fired half of everyone who had attended the event.

Here average-sized Dakota started to feel very afraid, for the Big Boss had a quick temper and could boil over on him any moment. "How will I ever manage this boss?" he thought. "He's only interested in showing his authority, firing workers every chance he gets! I can only wonder: how does anyone keep a job here?"

The Big Boss approached Dakota on his way to his turtle caddie and out of the blue said, "Have a nice day."

Dakota did not at all know what he meant by it, except the poor young man began to look for a path he could take to go home—that would make it a nice day—when he noticed a small white object shaking back and forth in midair behind a tree. It was a very curious thing at first but after coming nearer to it he determined it was a dog's tail and said to himself with great delight, "Why, it's the Westchester Whelp! She said she would meet me here."

"How's the game getting along?" the Westchester Whelp asked as soon as she came out from behind the tree.

"There you are, you little sneak," Dakota started, then suddenly checked himself because the dog began to spit out coffee beans. While Dakota waited until she finished, he thought, "There's no point in talking over her, for she might not hear me properly like last time." In another minute the dog stopped coughing, and Dakota put down his snake, which stayed where it was placed like a true golf club, and he summarized the happenings of the match, glad that the dog—his only friend here—had kept her promise of meeting him.

"I've never seen anything so absurd, never! They don't play fair, and their game has gone to the dogs!" Dakota complained, throwing his hands in the air. "With everything moving around, there really are poor playing conditions! First, there's the golf ball, an egg, which falls off the tee and rolls around, and then there are the clubs, which are slippery snakes, and one cannot get a good hold on them without gloves, nor keep them straight for very long." He crossed his arms, very upset. "And when all that's been figured out, and it's time to swing, everyone goes at it at once, without any rules for play or they make them up as they go—which makes them fight for no good reason—and the snakes swallow the eggs! It's all very confusing. I should have hit my egg, except my frog for a tee ran away!"

"And the weather?" the Whelp asked.

"Oh, it's unbearably hot! Like the dog days of summer!" Dakota whined.

"Well, I haven't gone mad, so it's not that hot. What do you make of your new boss?"

"I hate my boss," Dakota said angrily, "and I think he hates me and wants me to quit. He's such a bighead that—" Just then he heard the company and noticed the Big Boss walking behind him, so he changed course. "He has a very nice swing!"

The Big Boss smiled and waved him to continue along with them.

But the Chairman broke from the group and lumbered over to Dakota very oddly because of the chair stuck to his behind. "What are you doing?" he began in a sharp tone. "There's not a bird there you're talking to, is there? It is against the rules to talk to the birds."

At this Dakota remembered the Chairman's sly smile and thought, "He's covering for the Big Boss!" But he said, "No, I'm talking to my friend, a Westchester Whelp. Look for yourself." And Dakota moved to the side, so the dog came into the Chairman's view.

"You shouldn't be talking to any creatures. It is against the rules," the Chairman ordered in a severe manner. Then with a sudden change of heart he said, "Nice dog. It should be my caddie."

"Ha," the Westchester Whelp mocked. "*This* dog won't hunt."

Dakota looked to the Chairman for a tactful response, but he only stood there hunched over uncomfortably and processed the matter in silence. Soon the Chairman's ears became red, and with a fake smile he said, "Then you must be let go." He reached out to the Big Boss, who had gone only a few yards down the fairway. "This dog must be let go. She is not in compliance!"

The Big Boss had of course only one method to handle workers who did not respect the chain of command, or any matter not pleasing to him. "You're fired!" he shouted without stopping to think whom it was he was even firing.

"I don't work at your company," the Whelp barked.

"Well then, I'll just tell the boss of the golf course all the nasty things you said to me and have you fired," the Chairman said in a decided tone, and in another moment he hurried off in the opposite direction of the group and to the country club.

Dakota made up his mind to return to the game, as taking that route might lead him to a path in which he would not get in any more disputes. It was not hard to find which way the procession had gone, as he could hear the Big Boss screaming his favorite phrase. By the time he reached where they had all gathered, two workers had been fired and a pair of employees had taken the spots of the previously fired players, and the match was so much a mess that he skipped the rest of the swings and moved over to the hole and tried to guess which egg might be his as he waited for them.

The Eagle and Albatross were engaged in a squawking match—to see whose egg should be closer to the hole as the Birdie watched from a distance and laid another egg—which seemed like a good time for Dakota to practice his short game, except that his snake had slithered its way up a tree, where he could see it flicking its tongue at him.

By the end of half an hour or so, he had climbed up the tree and brought the snake down, the Eagle and Albatross had made a truce, and the three birds had fled the scene, so that he couldn't ask them which egg belonged to him. "Oh, what does it matter?" he lamented to himself. "All the eggs will be eaten anyway." He wrapped his snake club around his neck—so that he wouldn't leave it behind and lose it—and returned to his new best friend.

When he came upon the Westchester Whelp, the procession had crowded around, and the Drone, the Chairman, and the Big Boss discussed some matter which caused the others to look on with concerned faces. Dakota thought it'd be best for him to not get involved, so he settled on a plan of action to hide behind a nearby tree and listen closely.

But as he went into the rough for his hiding place, the Chief saw him and yelled for him to come over. Once Dakota arrived, they all appealed him to settle a dispute they were having about the dog and her future.

The Drone argued that you couldn't fire the dog for the sole reason she was not an employee of the company. Moreover, he stated that he had never done such a thing nor seen it be done in the history of employment.

The Chairman scoffed at this and argued that any being who was an employee of any organization could be fired by any separate entity, as long as it was happening from above, which then begged the question—the Big Cheese pointed this out—of income: if said employee had a higher salary than the Bigwig of another company, for example, could the Bigwig of that company fire him? And this puzzled all of them very deeply, so much that the conversation came to a halt for several minutes, and when one tried to start up the discussion, he or she lost his or her words and the group returned to thinking.

At last the Big Boss burst out with his sentiment: if they didn't come up with a solution in the next minute or two, he'd have everyone fired. To this those higher up on the Ladder of Diminishing Rungs—the original players excluding the Big Boss—quickly called for a vote, but it made no difference because it was a tie.

Just then a brilliant idea struck Dakota, so he said in a very weak voice (for, you see, with the current way of things he wasn't sure whether it would work), "The Bigwig owns the Westchester Whelp; why don't you ask her?"

"She's at home because of the investigation," the Big Boss said to the Drone. "Bring her here at once." And the Drone made like a bee and buzzed off.

The Whelp's tail slowed down until finally it stopped wagging altogether, and the happening was a most curious thing because in the next minute the tail turned into rock. And the animal sweated profusely and screamed a hysterical laugh, as though she had gone mad. By the time the Bigwig showed, the Whelp's whole body had hardened into a rock. "Dog my cats!" the Bigwig cried. "She's turned into a memorial stone." So each member of the company pulled out a tragedy mask and acted out a tragic farewell, and the Bigwig felt a little better because they all looked like they cared. Then the Big Boss announced without sympathy, "Who's up for some golf?" And the golf match picked up where it left off.

Chapter 10: The Plush Bear's Tragedy

"You don't know how much it means to the Bigwig that you came to her dog's funeral," the Bigwig said in a grateful yet melancholy voice as she hugged Dakota. Then she took his hand in hers, and they walked together to the next hole, holding hands.

Dakota was pleased to comfort her and glad that she was no longer talking about herself so arrogantly. It occurred to him that it was the caffeine that had made her anxious and bad-tempered when they met at the coffee shop.

"It was the work that killed her, you know," the Bigwig cried.

Dakota only humored the irony in her response as she continued to weep. "Applesauce! If I ever become a Bigwig," he thought, "I won't give coffee to my dog, not even for a buzz. For it wasn't the work that killed her, it was the coffee! One can work without—maybe it's *too much* coffee that made her sick. But I suppose too much of anything isn't good for you." He smiled to himself, having learned something new. "Too many greasy chips make people fat—and too much sugary soda gives you acne—and too much medicine causes side effects. If people knew that, they might save themselves a trip to the doctor."

Average-sized Dakota was so absorbed in his thoughts that he'd quite forgotten the Bigwig was deep in conversation with him, so when she clapped her hands in front of his face to snap him out of his head, he became startled.

"Are you even listening? The Bigwig just lost her dog!" she screamed, but after collecting herself she said in an apologetic tone,

"Oh, the Bigwig should've handled that better. It's just that she's not used to being in this position. First, she loses her chance to move up the Ladder of Diminishing Rungs—that's the only reason the Bigwig was in a relationship with the Big Boss—then she loses her dog. The Bigwig's a winner in every sense of the word, but next time she will be better and not lose her temper."

"Oh, it's okay. I sometimes lose my temper, too. Maybe there's nothing to improve," Dakota said, then came to a stop near a bench and sat down.

"Nonsense!" the Bigwig scoffed. "Everything can be improved, if you only take the time to see how it can be so." She plopped onto his lap and pressed her large breasts up against his face so that his eyes were level with them (for, you see, she was unaware that in his adult appearance there was as much deceit as in her mind; he was still ten years old). "It's the Bigwig's understanding that you have made it up the Ladder of Diminishing Rungs, and quite fast."

Here poor Dakota became bothered by her (for, you see, she was invading his personal space), and for three chief reasons: One, because the Bigwig had a lot of perfume, which made him want to sneeze. Two, because she had on several layers of makeup that made her look scary up close. And three, because she was a girl, and girls had cooties. Yet he did not want to be rude and push her away, so he waited until she left him on her own.

"The playing conditions seem to be improving," he pointed out, half hoping she might get off him and tend to the game.

"Of course they are," the Bigwig said. "There's always room for improvement."

"Speaking of rooms, this room is quite large," Dakota noted, remembering that the golf course was an office in the building.

"Yes, someone once said, 'The biggest room in the world is the room for improvement.'" Suddenly, the Bigwig pressed Dakota's face to her bosom and added, "You can enhance anything!"

"Holy seeds, she is preoccupied with improvement!" Dakota mumbled, stuck in the space between her breasts.

"You're probably wondering why the Bigwig hasn't improved the shining hour and dropped you her number." She adjusted herself on his lap so that he could breathe. "The reason is, the Bigwig was thinking that you might initiate, seeing that you're the man."

"I shouldn't have to," Dakota said.

"Very true," the Bigwig observed. "A woman should have courage and ask for what she wants! That would be an improvement. And an even better improvement, demand it! Then she'll get what she wants."

"I hardly think so."

"Perhaps if the Bigwig goes at it like a boy killing snakes?"

Just then the snake wrapped around Dakota's neck hissed, and he thought it might just attack her, but it only coiled itself around his neck once more. "I don't like snakes very much, but a boy who goes around killing snakes wouldn't make for a boy at all!"

The Bigwig looked at him, rather confused, then went on as before. "Darling, it really is cute of you to act virtuous. It can only mean one thing: you are hiding something. And like you, the Bigwig has a snake in her bosom, too." Dakota noticed his snake had moved its head down to his chest and flicked its tongue every other moment as she added, "It would be wise of the Bigwig to improve on her ethics, after all, it was why the Big Boss made her take a leave of absence."

"And why did he do that?" Dakota asked, eager to know the story that the Greenback Squirrel had started but never finished near the water cooler.

"If the Bigwig hadn't got caught cheating, he wouldn't have become as mad as a snake and acted the way he did." She sighed and said to herself in a subdued tone, "That is something else the Bigwig should improve on—not getting caught."

"Who are you trying to fool?" Dakota said. "I don't think you can be ethical and cheat at the same time!"

"Oh, but the Bigwig can," she said quite haughtily. "You see, the Bigwig wouldn't have gotten this far if she wasn't so clever. All it takes is wearing the right mask at the right time."

Here poor Dakota became thoroughly puzzled and said in a meek voice, "I don't understand why everyone here is so interested in wearing a mask and switching it every time something changes. Why can't anyone just be?"

"It is a sign of growth to be able to wear a mask without accepting it as yourself, that is, be whoever you want, or more simply, picture yourself to be someone other than what it might not look to others."

"I—I'm afraid I don't understand," Dakota said rather timidly. "But maybe I would if I was older."

"There's no need to fear the Bigwig," she stated in a soothing tone. "The Bigwig only wears a mask that makes her sound like she knows what she's saying."

"Please don't wear it again."

"Oh, don't tell the Bigwig what she should and shouldn't wear," the Bigwig said quite sharply. "With a wardrobe of a thousand masks, the Bigwig fools whoever she chooses. The Bigwig will make a mask of you and wear that, too."

"A mask that would make you look decent," Dakota thought, "I would be glad to see a mask like that!" But he kept this to himself so as not to offend her.

"Not listening again?" the Bigwig said as she shoved his face in her breasts.

"I don't have to listen to what I don't like," Dakota muttered.

"The same as only hear what you want. That's no improve—" The Bigwig suddenly trailed off on her favorite word—*improvement*—and jumped from Dakota's lap. He noticed the Big Boss had arrived, with his hands on his waist, ready to blow steam.

"A great day, dear boss," the Bigwig said, clearing her throat.

"Now that the funeral has ended, your time here with us is over," the Big Boss said sternly. "Either take your leave of absence, or be fired this instant! Choose wisely!"

The Bigwig stared at him for a moment, then hurried off without looking back.

In another minute the Big Boss wrapped his arm around Dakota in a friendly way and said, "Let us continue the round, shall we?"

Average-sized Dakota glanced at the man's arm, then his big head, and made up his mind to go along.

The other members of the party were playing and singing "Make-it-straight, Make-it-straight, Golfer's plan" (they were referring to their snakes for golf clubs) to the tune of "Pat-a-cake, Pat-a-cake, Baker's man" when the Big Boss and Dakota arrived; however, they quickly returned to the tournament, as the Big Boss complained that they were behind schedule and would need to pick up the pace or be fired.

As the golf match continued, the Big Boss repeatedly shouted, "You're fired!" to whoever played subpar—let their snakes fly without yelling *fore*. Those who were fired either left peacefully, which happened rarely, or thrashed their clubs, or sacks of snakes, and threw a hissy fit, so that by the end of the front nine, only Dakota, the

Chairman, and the Big Boss remained. As for the snakes, they slithered up the trees, and the caddies tried to bring them back.

The Big Boss concluded the game and declared himself victor, then headed for the country club—a horizontally long mansion with a statue of a bear in front of the entrance—and said to Dakota, "Do you know about the Plush Bear?"

"I have one at home," Dakota said fondly, remembering his fluffy friend.

"He hangs around the Bear Cave, works there part-time, now that he has nothing to do, being retired and all."

"I've never been to a cave," Dakota remarked in a weak voice, not sure he wanted to visit one.

"I bet we could catch him there. It is happy hour, after all. Follow me."

They entered the country club, and as they made their way around it, Dakota saw the Chairman in a room, which was actually a campsite, with all the players and guests who had been fired gathered around a campfire, roasting marshmallows and making s'mores, as they shared scary stories of how they were fired.

The Chairman patted a few of them on the back and informed the group, "None of you have been fired."

Dakota felt that was a good thing except it was not very nice of the Big Boss to scare everyone the way he had done.

The Big Boss led Dakota to a room, which was really a field of grass with mountains in the back, where a cow lay, wearing a dull gray suit jacket and a ten-gallon hat and drinking murky milk from a glass with crushed rocks and a mint leaf. The cow tipped her hat and said in a peculiar accent, "Howdy, y'all."

"Wipe your mouth, Milky!" the Big Boss said. The cow wiped her milk mustache. "And show this young man the Bear Cave and introduce him to the Plush Bear. I must freshen up, then get back to handling walking papers and pink slips for some workers I have fired."

"I'm fixing to head over there," Milky said at once.

Just before the Big Boss left, he added, "Oh, by the way, that's a nice jacket"—Dakota only saw the same dull gray suit jacket he and all the other creatures wore—to which Milky replied, "Thank you. I try to fit in." And the Big Boss disappeared, leaving Dakota with Milky.

Average-sized Dakota thought it nice to stay with Milky, for she was not threatening like the Big Boss, but was not quite sure whether to trust the cow to doing anything. The animal just sat, and sat, and sat some more, and setting aside the murky milk, moved her mouth in a circular fashion as she chewed on a piece of grass. So Dakota lay beside her and plucked at the blades of grass while he waited.

Once Milky finished the drink and wiped her mouth on her leg, she checked that no one was around and scoffed, "Bless his heart, the Big Boss and his threats to fire people. He always has a cow."

"Tell me about it." Dakota sighed.

"The Bear Cave's over yonder," Milky said, pointing with her snout. In another moment she stood on her hind legs, in the neighborhood of six feet, and turned in the direction of their destination. "You come here now." She started to lead him. "I reckon the Big Boss knows everything that happens around these parts, as if the eyes of Texas were upon you. He pretend-fires whoever doesn't meet his fancy, then walks around like a sacred cow, as if he never did anything wrong! All hat and no cattle if you ask me. It's just to mess with the workers, keep them on their toes."

"It seems everyone is about fear here," Dakota thought as he followed Milky up a stony path surrounded by trees and plants. "I don't think I've ever been so afraid, and it only happens when the Big Boss is around."

Before long they reached the Plush Bear, a six-foot-tall brown stuffed animal with a grizzled appearance, a bow tie, and a vest. He was sitting in the opening of a cave, leaning against the mountain. As they came closer, Dakota could see him drinking from a glass that had little rocks and gummy bears in it, or at least attempting to, for the plush toy could not actually take anything in by the mouth and had made quite a mess, spilling the drink on himself and the surrounding area. Dakota hankered to try some, as he liked gummy bears, and asked Milky, "What is he drinking?"

"It's a bear cocktail—bearbon with branch water, cider, honey, and gummies—and comes from that sketchy place outside Texas," Milky replied. "Since he retired, he hasn't stopped drinking, not even during work hours. Maybe he'll let you try some."

While Dakota imagined what the drink tasted like, Milky walked up to the Plush Bear, tipped her hat, and gently shook her glass back and forth, the crushed rocks rattling. "Another milk julep."

"Coming right up," the Plush Bear said in a fuzzy voice, then hiccupped and walked right under a wooden sign that had the words

Bear Cave carved into it with Dakota and Milky trailing. The teddy bear went behind a large rock that had been smoothed to a rough counter and had high rocks in front of it at which one could sit. Behind the counter were several bottles with labels on them, like bearbon, bearskey, bear ale, and so on.

While the Plush Bear picked out a pair of bottles and started to make the beverage, Dakota forgot all about his longing for the gummies, as a television overhead showed a program with puppets, a donkey and an elephant controlled by strings before a crowd of fat cats, and he exclaimed, "Ooh, a puppet show!"

The comment drew curious stares from the others, and Milky quickly corrected him in a contemptuous tone, "Politicians. Trust them as far as I can throw them!" Then she introduced Dakota to the teddy bear. "Why don't you tell this young man your life's *story*?"

"The days of *glory*? Moo over to them chairs"—the plush animal pointed with his nose and winked—"and I'll meet you there with the drink."

Milky laughed (for, you see, saying "moo" was an inside joke) and said, "Git-r-done!"

In another minute the Plush Bear came out from behind the counter with the cow's milk julep and his own bear cocktail and made his way to the stone armchairs and sofas where Milky and Dakota waited. "Where should I begin?"—he hiccupped—"Oh, yes, I was once a real bear named Grizzly." He shook his head and sighed.

This was followed by a long pause, as the Plush Bear stared into the distance, during which Milky finished her milk julep and kept making loud, sucking sounds to get whatever she could with the straw—Dakota found this to be rude—and the teddy bear hiccupped a few times. Dakota wanted to tell the plush animal to drink some water or hold his breath—if any of those were even possible—so that he could prevent the occasional hiccup, but kept to himself because it was quite funny to see a stuffed bear struggle with hiccups.

"When I was an athlete," the Plush Bear said at last, which was interrupted by a hiccup, "we had to bear a lot of training. That's how I became successful."

"Holy seeds, an athlete!" Dakota's eyes shone with wonder, as he hoped to become some kind of athlete one day, maybe a baseball or football star. "I want to do well in sports, too. Did you have a coach?"

"Do bears poop in the woods?" the Plush Bear said in a sarcastic sort of way. "You clearly have little experience."

"Come on, new guy, we can't go on explaining everything to you," Milky added, breaking from her annoying sucking sounds with the milk julep. In another moment she and the Plush Bear looked at each other and shook their heads in disgust, which made average-sized Dakota feel embarrassed. Then Milky urged, "Get on with the *story*."

"Yes, the *glory*," the Plush Bear started, then hiccupped. "I achieved many feats, many of which you will never accomplish."

"I too can accomplish them," Dakota barked, without considering so much as what it was the teddy bear competed in.

"He's tenacious," Milky remarked, putting her drink down on the ground. "That's sure enough a sign of success."

The Plush Bear yawned and said, rather condescendingly, "That may be good for certain things. Not for sleeping very long."

"Oh, but when I sleep, I crash," Dakota said eagerly. "On the weekends, I can go for twelve hours—that's half the day right there. So you need not be very proud of that."

"Can you hibernate for months on end?"

"No," Dakota muttered.

"Then you'll never win the annual Hibernation Champion award, which I have won every year since I left school up until retirement," the Plush Bear said very arrogantly, then attempted to sip his drink, which of course only made a mess.

Here Dakota wondered aloud, "When did sleeping become a competition?"

The Plush Bear continued, "But I was good at other sports, too. What about you?"

"Oh, yes, I'm very good at all of them. I can—" Dakota was about to say he could throw a football with a perfect spiral and dribble a basketball fluidly with either hand, and go on about his skills, but the Plush Bear interrupted him with a hiccup and asked, "What about snatching?"

"I've never heard of snatching," Dakota said, thoroughly puzzled. "What is it?"

Suddenly, Milky's head bobbed forward, and she opened her mouth wide. "That's a kicker! You don't know about snatching? But you've heard of fishing, haven't you?"

"Yes, it's when you use a rod and catch fish," Dakota answered.

"Then how can you not have heard of snatching?" Milky said, astonished. "They are almost the same sport; the only difference, I reckon, is you might would use a claw instead of a rod in a tank. Clearly, you just fell off the turnip truck, new guy."

Dakota ventured to bend the truth, so he would sound knowledgeable and Milky would stop calling him *new guy*, and said, "Oh, when I use my hand, I call it fishing, and—"

"Call it what you like, it's still snatching," Milky said in a serious tone. To this the Plush Bear nodded, and Dakota checked himself before saying something ugly in return.

"How often do you catch fish?" the Plush Bear asked, then took up his beverage to only add to the spill he had made.

"Whenever I go," Dakota replied, glad to get an opportunity to show off his little fortune. "I even have a trophy to show for my excellence. My dad taught—"

"Well, I caught fish every day," the Plush Bear interrupted, "not just whenever I went, and I was so good, there's even a statue of me in this building, on the golf course. And a statue is better than a trophy." The teddy bear smiled quite pompously, then hiccupped, which made him look silly.

Here Dakota sighed and lost interest in the conversation; the Plush Bear had an annoying tendency to one-up him whenever he could. And Dakota thought, "Why is he so proud, so arrogant? Maybe the praise and fame—yes! He thinks about them all the time. That's all his head is filled with. It's a great wonder his head hasn't swollen to that of the Big Boss's. One can be quite rude when—maybe success really can go to one's head!"

At any rate Dakota wanted to leave (for, you see, he found the Plush Bear to be very rude, blowing his own trumpet), but he made up his mind to hear the end of the stuffed animal's story and asked in a humoring sort of way, "What other things were you good at?"

"There's climbing," the Plush Bear replied, then continued with the occasional hiccup, "and treeology—you have to have a good knowledge of all the trees if you're going to climb them and be successful at it."

"And know the bark," Milky intervened.

"That's if you want to be good at scratching your back against the tree," the Plush Bear continued. "I hold the record for twelve times. Then there's caving—you get to do that if you show good behavior and are responsible—in which you patrol the caves as a cave monitor, you know, for predators, troublemakers, stuff like that. They give you a vine to wear as a sash."

"What is that like?"

"You should ask Milky; I was nowhere near as good as her." With that, the stuffed animal returned to the bear cocktail.

Dakota thought, "At last he is not good at something," and he nearly swooped in and lied that he had been a hall monitor, a position he sorely wanted at school, just so he could stick it to the Plush Bear, but Milky began before he could let out a word.

"What can I say," Milky said with an air of bravado, blowing air on her humanlike hands. "I can see nearly all around me and sense when a predator is coming from every direction. I've won multiple Field Monitor awards because of it. Y'all see this bell?"—she pointed to the bell around her neck—"It's one of my medals. Git-r-done!"

"Were you an athlete, too?" Dakota asked Milky.

"Not quite, but I played sports. I showed an early interest for making things, so I became an inventor."

"What do you invent?"

"Milk, ice cream, cheese, yogurt, butter—all the profitable stuff," Milky replied. "Heck, you might as well call me a cash cow."

"And how did the Plush Bear become what he is today?" Dakota asked, eager to finish the stuffed animal's story before Milky started on her own.

Just then the Plush Bear looked away and brought his brows together, as though he didn't want to go on, so Milky swooped in and made quick work of the story. "Well, some time when Plushy was on top of the world, he slipped off a branch during climbing practice and fell forty feet and broke his back and legs! The fall was uglier than sin. Couldn't bear to watch it, terrible thing it was."

"Holy seeds," Dakota said, putting his hand over his mouth. "That must have hurt."

"It did," the Plush Bear muttered, then went back to looking away and crossed his arms.

Milky continued, "He recovered—not right quick but a while— then he returned to the games, but he was never quite the same. The next generation, which he had taught, had surpassed him, and they started breaking all the records he had set."

"Then what happened?" Dakota pressed. This was all very interesting yet depressing at the same time.

"Well, he kept on trying to compete, but you've got to know when to hold them and when to fold them. So after a few years of losing, he hung it up. Now he only participates for charitable causes," Milky said, then took a moment to pick up the milk julep and make loud, sucking sounds while she tried to get whatever was left of it with her straw. "We tried to cheer him up before the next Hibernation Games and invited him to Thanksgiving dinner. And then—" She looked at the teddy bear. "Dad gum it, why don't you finish the *story*? I can't remember all that happened."

"But there is no more *glory*," the stuffed animal muttered.

"Everything after that part—how you came to be known as Plushy," Milky said, shaking her head.

The Plush Bear sighed. "Every year I look forward to Thanksgiving, my favorite holiday. It's the one day I can see all my friends and family."

"Oh, yes, I love holidays," Dakota said at once. "My favorite is Halloween because—"

"Yes, well, that one is okay, but I say it's not the best holiday, nor a holiday at all." The Plush Bear hiccupped. "But anyway, every Thanksgiving I'm hungry, but this time, because I was feeling low, I was hungry as a bear."

"What other kind of hungry could you get?" Dakota thought, then said, "Oh, yes, I get very hungry, too, on that day."

"But I was hungrier than the average bear."

"Oh, yes, I am like that as well."

"Well, I was so hungry that it was more than one can bear."

"Oh, that is quite hungry," Dakota observed and let the matter go. The Plush Bear was doing it again—trying to prove he was the best. And Dakota pitied the stuffed animal for it occurred to him: "Why, his whole life is based on what he accomplished or didn't accomplish."

Then to tickle the Plush Bear's fancy, he said, "Well, you must be the hungriest bear there ever was."

"Yes." Just then the Plush Bear paused, momentarily appeased. "So when I went to Milky's dinner party, the table was lined with all the bare necessities, like cranberry casserole, and, and pumpkin sauce, and, and green bean pie"—he kept licking his lips and rubbing his hands together—"and corn potatoes, and macaroni and gravy, and, and turkey rolls, and mashed—"

Dakota faintly recognized the food items and ventured to correct him. "I think you mean mashed potatoes, and cranberry sauce, and pumpkin pie, and . . . well, I forgot what else you mentioned. It was quite a list."

"Yes, it was a lot, but no, I mean what I said," the Plush Bear stated confidently.

"I'm afraid you're messing up the recipes," Dakota argued just as certain.

"Please bear in mind, you didn't bear witness to *my* Thanksgiving. It's my story. What do you know?" In another moment the Plush Bear crossed his arms and gave Dakota the silent treatment, which of course came with the occasional hiccup.

"Oh, please don't be angry. I was only trying to help," poor Dakota said, very sorry.

After a minute or so, the Plush Bear reluctantly said, "Well, I suppose I could grin and bear it."

Dakota was delighted to hear that; he settled on a plan of action to not correct the stuffed animal's story, no matter how absurd it sounded, and said in an encouraging tone, "Oh, yes, please do go on."

"Okay, as I was saying"—the Plush Bear hiccupped—"mashed insects, and honey salmon, and, and squash with beet, carrot, and radish stuffing, and, and grass bread, and my personal favorite, dead flesh and berry salad."

Here Dakota began to see that the stuffed animal had an entirely different experience than his own (for, you see, the latter food items were common to a bear's diet).

"When I saw the food," the Plush Bear continued, "I couldn't help myself. I touched it and burned my finger." He showed his humanlike paw; a small burn marked it. "It was hot enough to burn a polar bear's butt."

At this Dakota slapped his knee and laughed. "A polar bear's butt?"

"It's not funny, you know," the Plush Bear said in a solemn tone. "One of my uncles is a polar bear, and it really hurts."

"Oh, I'm sorry, I thought you were trying to be funny," Dakota said innocently.

"If I was trying to be funny, I would've told you I had a joke." Just then the six-foot-tall Plush Bear showed his teeth, a thin strip of felt.

After the initial shock that comes from such an experience went away, average-sized Dakota said, glad to be the adult in the conversation, "Please don't bare your teeth. It's very rude." In another moment he was surprised to find himself talking like the stuffed animal and added in a decided tone, "I'm not saying any more."

They sat quietly for some minutes while the Plush Bear hiccupped and Milky made sucking sounds with her straw. In the meantime Dakota's longing to leave returned, and he considered once or twice to get up and be gone like the wind but made up his mind that he would stay, for he had nowhere else to go, and only agree with the stuffed animal being that he was quite sensitive. Soon he became impatient and asked, "Now what?"

"Now, as I was saying," the Plush Bear began at last, "I was as cross as a bear because I had to wait for the food to cool down before I could eat it."

"Oh, yes, I would be, too," Dakota said, pleased to see the Plush Bear start up again.

"I couldn't bear watching the other bears, the older ones, munching and chomping. I kept thinking there would be none left."

"Oh, yes, I would be worried, too. Then what happened?"

"Well, after a while, the food cooled, and I stuffed myself, and stuffed some more, and stuffed again, thinking that eating would make me feel better and prepare me for the Hibernation Games. The others warned me to stop—even tried to wrestle the food away from me. I felt my hair turning fluffy, but I stuffed and stuffed until I became a stuffed animal!"

Here Dakota drew his face into a puzzled look, for he was not sure whether he should feel sorry for the teddy bear or laugh; it was all just so curious. But seeing the Plush Bear looking down in a dejected sort of way, Dakota pitied the poor stuffed animal and gave him a bear hug.

"Now my heart doesn't beat like it used to," the Plush Bear muttered.

But Dakota didn't hear a heartbeat at all. And he thought, "Well, now his heart has stopped, so I don't know how he goes on. Maybe he is dead. Holy seeds, what if it is possible to die before dying? Then how—that might be possible if one lets failure get to one's heart."

Dakota brooded on this matter in silence as they finished hugging and he returned to the stone sofa.

"That's enough stories for the day," Milky said in a decided tone. "Tell him about the happy hour team-building exercises."

Chapter 11: The Cave Painting

The Plush Bear finished his bear cocktail, or rather making a mess, then hiccupped and looked confused. He opened his mouth to speak but couldn't until a series of hiccups passed.

"Same as a bump in the road," Milky commented; and she at once set about taking away the stuffed animal's keys and glass.

At last the Plush Bear stopped hiccupping and shook his head. Just then his fuzzy voice became hurried and careless. "I bet you haven't been in a cave before."

To which Dakota replied, "I haven't."

"So I gather you've never seen a cave painting."

Dakota almost interrupted with, "I've painted in art class," but said, "Not yet."

"So you have no understanding of the ancient art of art!"

"I guess I don't," Dakota said. "What is the ancient art of art?"

"The first matter of course," Milky said, "is to grab some rocks."

"Gemstones!" the Plush Bear cried. "It would be good of you to pick them up, like red and green, blue and black, purple and—"

"It takes some time to find these rocks," Milky interrupted.

"But better ingredients make for a better painting," the teddy bear said. "We've got some pails filled with gemstones behind the counter."

"Then there's the flat surface in the cave you might would need," Milky said.

"That's another one of the ingredients," the teddy bear added.

"Make groups of three. Normally, we have more people—"

"Lucky for you, we'll have to leave the competition part out," the teddy bear yelled. "My team would have beaten yours."

"And stand in a line near the wall—"

"But not too close," the stuffed animal shouted, then back to his indistinct tone, "That might make it hard to see the big picture."

"The one you're painting," Milky made clear. "Then the Woodpecker times everything."

"It's good to set an appointment with him," the Plush Bear said, shaking his head again—the bear cocktail had indeed gotten to him—"like I did for today. His schedule is very busy."

"The participants begin painting at once, and when time's up, everyone votes—"

"You can't vote for your own," the plush toy screamed, then in a subdued tone, "The rules should be changed."

"—for the best cave painting, and when it's all said and done, we clear the paintings—except the winner's—by spitting water on them."

"That's why there are so few cave paintings," the Plush Bear explained.

"It must be a very fun painting exercise," Dakota remarked.

"Would you like to participate?" the teddy bear asked.

"I sure would," Dakota said with great delight.

"Wait right here, and I'll get the stones!" the Plush Bear said eagerly. In another moment he set off for the counter, and Dakota watched him, half curious and half alarmed, for he walked in anything but a straight line, swaying back and forth all the way. He returned in the same manner but with two buckets of gemstones while Milky sought out a smooth wall in the cave.

"We can do without gemstones, you know, but it would be rather dull," the cow said.

"Yes, it would," Dakota said, "like a pencil draw—"

"I'm good at painting and using my claws to add a 3-D effect," the Plush Bear stated, then turning to Milky he asked, "What are your core competencies?"

"I might will can do the same, except the clawing part, I reckon," Milky answered.

"The both of you can work together. I'll make my own painting over here," Dakota said in a decided tone, off to the side. "And we can vote who won."

"What's his problem?" Milky asked the stuffed animal rather sharply.

"The new guy thinks he's better than us," the Plush Bear said in an offended tone.

To which Dakota almost replied, "I do not!" but before he could say a word, Milky burst out in a very nasty sort of way, "Can you say weirdo?"

"Not a team player. That's a career-limiting move, a weakness to be worked on," the Plush Bear mocked.

"A good reason to be fired, I reckon," Milky said.

They kept teasing poor average-sized Dakota for some time until he at last succumbed to their taunts. "How rude!" he thought. "I've never been so bullied, never. Oh, they are lucky an adult isn't here, for I would tattle on them at once, and oh, just think how much trouble they would get in! Come, I'll show them who's a team player."

In another moment or two, Dakota calmed down and thought, "How is going at it alone a weakness? Applesauce! Painting is not a group activity anyway. I've never seen such a thing, never. They should—holy seeds, it's quite easy to lose one's independence in Corporate America. I don't think I like teamwork much, certainly not like this." And Dakota suddenly had an aha moment: "There is no *I* in team."

"Good, you've finally come to your senses," the Plush Bear said once Dakota committed to paint with them. "Because you think you're so good at this—'Look at me, I can make my own painting'—you can paint with Milky while I sing you the directions."

Dakota was not sure how a painting had directions but remained silent and followed orders to avoid being made fun of again.

"Woodpecker!" the Plush Bear shouted toward the exit. "Begin at once."

In another minute the Woodpecker started pecking, so it sounded like a timer, and the Plush Bear started to sing very slowly (for, you see, he had too much to drink) to the tune of "If You're Happy and You Know It."

"If you see a blue stone, take it out!
If you see a blue stone, take it out!
If you have a blue stone, then you'll surely paint and shout
If you see a blue stone, take it out!

Okay, everyone, now we are going to grab another color
Get ready. Here we go.

If you see a red stone, take it out!
If you see a red stone, take it out!
If you have a red stone, then you'll surely paint and shout
If you see a red stone, take it out!"[1]

(During the first part, with the blue stone, Milky mooed and the Plush Bear roared on cue while Dakota watched. When the time came to make a noise again, Dakota shouted, gaining familiarity with the lyrics, and with a great smile.)

The song went on like this—with the occasional argument when one of them picked up the wrong stone—until they had exhausted the range of colors you see in a rainbow. They had a gemstone for each of the seven shades, but the rocks failed to produce the intended effect.

Average-sized Dakota found himself singing along and having a good time during happy hour—it was a combination of art and choir—though the painting turned out to be nothing he could readily make out, with so many stone and claw marks all over the place.

"Thank you, the painting exercise is fun to be a part of," Dakota said, wishing it would go on a little longer. "But what is the painting supposed to be?"

"It is a cat of course," the Plush Bear said as though it were all very obvious, "a mountain lion. You've seen one, haven't you?"

"Oh, yes, at the zzz—" Dakota suddenly checked himself before saying "zoo" for fear the animals might not find it agreeable that they were kept behind cages, like the Black Rat.

"I've never been to Zzz," the Plush Bear remarked. "Will have to add it to the territories that need to be taken over. If you've seen mountain lions, you must know what they're like?"

"Of course I do," Dakota replied, glad to have a chance to show off the little things he knew. "They're carnivores and live on mountains, and you should call for help if you see one, because they can be threatening."

---

[1] Derivative of "A Color Chorus" by Angela Thayer (2014). See www.teachingmama.org for original song.

Sameer Garach

"Yes, you've got that all right, especially that threatening part," the Plush Bear said. "We don't like them competing with our company, so we give them a generous offer to buy the land—more fish than the land's worth. And they always have doubts to take the offer and move out, so they—" Here the Plush Bear's eyes moved in opposite circles, dizzy. "Finish the explanation," he said to Milky.

"So they purr," Milky said. "Because they're never sure whether they might should give up their territory for fish—it's not part of their diet. And they say *purr* because they might will can't say the *haps* part, as in, *perhaps*. It's a little bit like me; that's why I always say *moo* when I want things to go."

"Is this all true?" Dakota asked rather doubtfully.

"You can hang your hat on it," Milky replied.

"Holy seeds!" Dakota fixed his gaze on the cow, intrigued yet confused by how animals communicated. "Now I know to move when I hear a cow moo. I never have learned so much about words."

"I have more to say about such things; this ain't my first rodeo," Milky added. "Do you know what you're trying to say when you say *hmm*?"

"No, I'm afraid I don't," Dakota replied in a meek voice. "I don't think I'm trying to say anything."

"You are trying to say *hump*, but the *p* doesn't come out," Milky said.

Dakota had never thought about "hmm" like that before. "A'lesauce! I can say hum—hum—" Suddenly, he became frustrated and surprised at the same time, not able to express himself the way he wanted. It was a most curious thing to have the right word in his head and for it to not come out right.

"See, you mean one thing, but might will say another," Milky said in a decided tone. "When you say *hmm*, you are reflecting or hesitating, stuck on something, no?"

"Why, yes, I *hmm* because I can't figure something out, or I have doubts and hold back," wise Dakota answered.

"Then you are trying to get over a hump," Milky explained.

Dakota thought about this a good deal before responding. "But I can't, so I say hum—I mean hum—" He brought his brows together and tried very hard, but, alas, it just wouldn't work, and so he sighed.

"Purrs and moos and hmms are failed attempts to say the right words," Milky said, "and though you might could have good intentions,

115

it doesn't come out the way you thought it might would. And the learning in that is that you have no control."

"New guys always think they have control," the Plush Bear remarked, "but it doesn't work like that in Corporate America. My advice: only try to control what you can."

Just then Dakota remembered the cave painting: the outcome could have been better. "The picture might have looked like a mountain lion if I was in charge," he said very sure of himself, "because I would have given out roles, like 'you, paint a head' and 'you, make a tail,' and so on."

"But these are the rules," the Plush Bear said sternly. "No employee can get around them."

"You could bend them, couldn't you?" Dakota said in a weak voice.

"That's not possible! Why, if an employee came to me and told me he was going to do whatever he wanted, I would've said, 'Know your role!'"

Here Dakota turned silent and thought, "They all take a fancy to rules here." In another moment he recalled the Cuckoo Bird's patchy fable about the corporate hierarchy and wondered how anyone could find freedom following so many rules, being a "team player."

"All these rules seem unnecessary, and yet they prefer it that way!" he said to himself, then to the others in a daring sort of way, "Maybe some rules are meant to be broken."

"You go on and do that," the Plush Bear said, "see how that turns out. It's you who will get broken."

And Milky added, "I reckon we've got ourselves a cowboy here! You might could be holding on to something bitter. Now, go on, sugar, tell us what's keeping you up at night."

"I could tell you everything I'm not happy with—starting with my appearance," Dakota said in a sorrowful tone. "But there's no use in wanting to look as I once did, because that time has passed."

"Lie down and tell us how you feel." The Plush Bear pulled out a notebook and pen from his vest's pocket.

"Express yourself and do it good," Milky said in a soothing tone. In another moment she put on a pair of glasses and added, "Then you won't need help from anybody else."

So Dakota lay on the rocky sofa and started talking about his frustrations with the New World from the time he followed the

Greenback Squirrel down hopscotch lane. He was afraid to be judged at first, the two of them acting very strange—the Plush Bear writing notes and Milky listening very intently—but he pushed on, as they hadn't said anything rude. His shrinks asked a few questions to understand his anxieties, then stopped him after he said he couldn't sing "I Look in the Mirror" to the Mask in the Looking Glass all proper and with the joy that normally accompanies music.

The Plush Bear clicked his pen closed and remarked, "That really is sad."

"As sad as one can get, I reckon," Milky followed.

"It came out all depressing!" the Plush Bear said. "Maybe you had a bad moment, or a few, not a bad day."

"I smell what you're stepping in," Milky said, "but you're gonna have to carry on, come hell or high water."

"Let's try singing something new." The teddy bear looked at the cow and raised his brows as though he were expecting her to come up with a song.

"Sit up and give 'The Little Brown Duck' a go," Milky ordered.

"The animals sure have many requests for songs," Dakota thought. "It's like sitting around the campfire all over again." Nevertheless, he sat up and started at once, but his head was so filled with the day's frustrations, he remembered the lyrics with some difficulty and the song came out rather funny:

"There's a little brown boy, standing in the tree trunk
A little brown boy, wondering where he sunk
He took some medicine he had
Grew his body tall and he said, 'I'm sad'
I'm a tall brown boy standing in the tree trunk
Help, help, help, help, help, help, help!"

Just then Milky brought her humanlike hand up to stop Dakota and remarked, "That's all very curious and depressing."

"And that's all about you, isn't it? I dare say it's an ego problem," the Plush Bear said rather condescendingly.

"He's incredibly stupid!" Dakota thought. "I should think he has the ego problem, what with all his nonsense about being better than the rest. He should check himself before saying such things." In another moment poor Dakota lay back down and looked at the cave ceiling, wondering why suddenly everything was about him and music could not lift his spirits.

"There are many things," the Plush Bear said, "bottled up inside of you that are wanting release."

"He can't express himself," Milky said. "That's the problem. Try the next stanza but with more energy."

"But about him taking medicine?" the Plush Bear asked rather doubtfully. "How could it make him sad?"

"I wasn't at first," average-sized Dakota explained, "except that after I became thin and unsteady, I was."

"Anyhow, keep going," Milky pushed impatiently.

Dakota went through the lyrics in his head, hoping they might come out right, though with the way everything had been, he was quite sure they wouldn't, and so his voice trembled:

"There's a tall brown boy walking in the street
A tall brown boy, trying to find his way in the heat
He took another medicine he had
That would shrink his hair and he said, 'I'm sad'
I'm a short-haired brown boy walking in the green
Help yelp, help yelp, help yelp, yelp!"

"Comes out the same as before, as if he was losing his memory," the Plush Bear remarked. "No expression, only frustrations. It's the most terrible thing I've ever heard."

"I reckon you might should better get some help, like from the company therapist," Milky recommended.

Here poor Dakota wondered whether he would get the opportunity to actually see the doctor, for he was quite certain that Dr. Quack would remain a mystery.

"You liked the Cave Painting, so I reckon you might will want to go at it again," Milky continued. "Or—yee-haw, here come the employees!" At that moment the workers poured into the Bear Cave, sat on the high rocks near the counter, and began shouting orders over one another—"Bearbon on the rocks over here!—Bearskey sour, chop-chop!"—and so on—to the Plush Bear, who had already gone off to manage the customers. Milky started heading there and looked over her shoulder to Dakota. "You come here now."

"Oh, yes, the creatures I've met!" Dakota said, seeing that the crowd had many recognizable faces, such as the Drone and White Mouse (the Mouse had slipped out of his pajamas and into a dull gray suit jacket).

"You're just in time for the 'Happy Hour Song,'" Milky said. "It's the perfect way to express your feelings."

Average-sized Dakota moved to one of the high rock stools near the counter and wedged himself between Milky and the Greenback Squirrel. He looked all around him: Smiles and stories marked the merry gathering, and the Plush Bear served mugs filled with what seemed to be sparkling apple juice or root beer. Moreover, Dakota saw a bunch of animals drinking from glass bottles like the ones he'd seen his dad drink out of after work and at parties from time to time.

In another minute or two, they broke into the song:

"We feel sick, our job's a joke
But we can't quit, we might go broke
At the end of the day, we can't think
But we earned our pay, so now we drink

We drink and get dizzy; we drink and get dizzy
We drink and get dizzy; we drink and get dizzy

We came in tired, faces with frowns
We'll leave inspired, our lips upside down
During work, we don't blend
But after work, we're all friends

We drink and get dizzy; we drink and get dizzy
We drink and get dizzy; we drink and get dizzy

This is the happy hour, the day is about to be over
No more being sour, let's lose our loafers
Our problems grow, a drink does the trick
Flushed down the throat, it gives us a kick

We drink and get dizzy; we drink and get dizzy
We drink and get dizzy; we drink and get dizzy

Don't mention tomorrow, around the corner
It grows our sorrow, and makes us mourners
Order another round, today's all that matters
Twist off the crown, and let's all gather

We drink and get dizzy; we drink and get dizzy
We drink and get dizzy; we drink and get dizzy

Don't post photos, our boss won't like it
He'll fire those, who got too excited
Stories will be told, short and long
Pop the cork, and sing along!"

Here Dakota joined the group and sang the only words he knew—the chorus—with great delight, then the workers went on without him. The Greenback Squirrel passed Dakota a mug filled with little rocks and sparkling liquid, and after one good look at the curious beverage it occurred to him that the drink was certain to disagree with him sooner or later (for, you see, there had been too many side effects from everything he had taken).

"Empty the jug, it's time for the buzz
Now tip that mug, and chug, chug, chug!"

In the next moment Dakota ignored his worries and started with a sip and remarked, "Oh, I just love it!"

To which the Squirrel said with a great, big smile, "So don't I."

Finding the drink agreeable, Dakota drank and drank, as the others sang and danced. The beverage tasted like apple cider but came with a most strange kick. The cider was very strong, and whatever sweetness it should have, it didn't. Soon after he finished the mug and wiped the resultant mustache with his sleeve, he became dizzy and the others around him started to multiply. Doubles and triples of the same creature appeared, and Dakota thought the merry little gathering had turned into a party.

"Dad gum it, happy hour is over. Back to work *right* quick!" Milky cried, and the employees stopped their singing and dancing and drinking at once.

"What do we *write*?" Dakota mumbled.

"The rank-and-yank is starting!" someone yelled from outside the Bear Cave.

"Moo!" Milky said hastily to Dakota.

In another moment average-sized Dakota rose, so fast that he nearly fainted, and when he at last recovered himself and tried to walk away from the rock stool, he stepped left, then right, and began to tumble to the floor before Milky caught him. "What's a rank-and-yank?" he asked, his speech hurried and careless like the Plush Bear's.

But Milky only replied, "Moo!" and she and the Squirrel wrapped Dakota's arms around their necks and skedaddled—leaving the Plush Bear to clean up and sing alone.

Dakota and the American Dream

Chapter 12: Which Muppet Must Go?

The Chairman and Big Boss were seated under a large pergola, a structure made of posts and decorated with curtains and climbing plants and vines, on a terrace garden on top of the building when Dakota and his carriers arrived, with the workers—all sorts of creatures—in open work spaces and small partitioned-off areas, as well as the original players from the golf tournament in their respective offices, smaller pergolas.

Outside the large structure, the Greenback Squirrel was at his log desk—which had a cannon parked right next to it—with a banana to his ear, talking away while eating some acorns from a bowl and resting his legs on the table, and the Chief and Big Cheese stood outside their offices and kept an eye on everyone.

In the middle of the open work area was a cake. It looked so good from afar that it made average-sized Dakota quite hungry. "I wish they'd hurry up with this yank-and-rank," he thought, "and serve the cake!" He made his way over to the sweet, and his eyes fell upon the writing on the cake: "No one will miss you, muppet!"

At this Dakota shuddered and backed away (for, you see, he had never seen such a rude farewell message). In spite of that, to his great delight he was finally at the top of the octopus-shaped skyscraper, and though he would have liked to walk around the edges and marvel at the surrounding buildings and clouds, he scarcely had any time to appreciate where he was, for there were too many things happening before his eyes.

Dakota and the American Dream

Dakota had never visited a workplace before but had seen them in cartoons and movies, and he was pleased to find that he had some knowledge of the things present. "I think that's their version of a boardroom," he said to himself, looking at the large structure, "because it has a huge table—I mean log—and lots of chairs—stumps—for a meeting!"

In another moment he turned to a small partitioned-off area and noted, "And that's a cubicle because the walls make a cube!"

The cubicle, to be clear, was made of lush walls of greenery, about half the size of Dakota, so that he had a good overview of the peculiar terrace office, like the Chief and Big Cheese.

"And those are computers," Dakota observed, "and they're used to get work done by the animals—no, employees." It was important for him to use the right language to describe the creatures because he was in an office. And he repeated the last word to himself a few times, pleased that he knew how to address them properly. However, "workers" would have been just as good.

The employees were all working very busily at their workstations, or it appeared that way at first. But upon closer examination, the typing on the keyboards turned out to be random punching, and the writing on the papers, pictures. Dakota found the whole matter to be absurd and said to Milky, quite astonished, "They're not doing anything! Only fake typing on the computers and doodling on the papers."

"Shh, don't blow their cover," Milky scolded. "It's not important to be busy but to appear busy. That's all the Big Boss might will sees, and what he might will sees is all he might will knows."

"How misleading!" Dakota started to let out his frustration rather loudly, which caused quite a stir, as many employees in the cubicles popped their heads up like prairie dogs. But he reined in his tongue, for the Greenback Squirrel broke from the conversation on the banana phone and cried, in his peculiar accent, "Quiet please! There's a meeting in progress."

The Chairman stood—though his chair never left his behind—and examined the area outside the boardroom to determine who was causing a ruckus.

Dakota turned away quickly to the open work space and looked over an employee's shoulder, as though he and the employee were working on something together. "Just have to keep pretending!" he said to himself, frustrated. When he viewed the others around him, all of the employees were hitting their keyboards quite stupidly—one poor creature didn't so much as have the monitor turned on. "Applesauce! Can't even pretend to look busy!" Dakota thought, then sighed.

One of the employees—the White Mouse—had started doodling on itself with a black fountain pen. This of course had to be discouraged, for Dakota could not stand the ridiculousness of it happening under his nose, and he at once went over to the rodent's cubicle and got behind him. In another moment he took a white-out pen from the log desk and quickly switched the pens. He did it so fast that the poor White Mouse didn't even realize what had happened. So after finding that nothing had changed, and determining that he should get back to looking busy, he began to doodle on himself with the white-out pen; and this of course corrected his fur to the right color.

The Chairman picked up a banana from the log table in the boardroom and talked into it, loud enough for the others to hear. "Acting Assistant to the Big Boss, call in the Fiscal Feline."

At this the Greenback Squirrel picked up the banana on his own log desk and yelled, "Lion, pick up your phone!"

The Fiscal Feline whisked away flies from his face with his tail, then answered his phone—the bone of some animal—and shouted back, "Yes, I'm here."

Then the Greenback Squirrel went on as before, "The Big Boss and Chairman would like to review your performance at this hour."

The Fiscal Feline hung up his phone slowly—placed the bone back down on his log desk—and adjusted his top hat and bow tie. He walked to the boardroom while holding his tail and mumbling, very nervous.

"They're incredibly stupid!" Dakota thought, for it was quite silly to use objects for phones when they clearly didn't have any effect.

"Prepare the cake and walking papers, I mean, napkins!" the Chairman said over the banana to the Greenback Squirrel.

The Fiscal Feline came into the boardroom holding his tail and said in a meek voice, "Hey, Boss, I mean bosses, how's everything?"

The leaders stared the cat down for some time while he sweated, then at last the Chairman began in a serious tone, "The Creature Company is not doing well, so we have decided to go in a different direction. Part of that involves downsizing, which means we have to fire someone today, and that someone is you."

The Fiscal Feline glanced at the Big Boss, speechless, then returned to the Chairman and argued in a trembling voice, "Well, hold on now, I—"

"We've reviewed your meetings. Quite frankly, they fail to move the needle," the Chairman said.

"Well, I'll take it to the next level, be more productive, you know, hold more of them," the Fiscal Feline pleaded, "at nights, weekends, whenever I can."

"No, I'm sorry. These meetings you hold," the Chairman said, "it's almost as if you have no business training at all. I don't see what impact they have on the company."

"I was just trying to look busy," the Fiscal Feline muttered.

"I'm sorry, we just can't keep you on board," the Chairman said politely, but in another moment he added in a severe tone, "Give us your name tag!"

"You don't want to fire me," the Fiscal Feline ventured to say.

Just then the Chairman turned to the Big Boss and asked, very confused, "We don't?" The Big Boss only shrugged, so the Chairman said, "Maybe we don't."

"You want to fire someone else," the Fiscal Feline said rather wisely, "like the Gorilla. I'm so much better at my job than the 800-pound Gorilla. All he does is throw his weight around."

Here the Big Boss leaned closer with his big head, so that it towered over the Fiscal Feline, and narrowed his eyes on the cat, who put his tail between his legs.

"Give us one good reason why we shouldn't fire you," the Chairman demanded, "and remove your tail from between your legs. It's very un-lionlike!"

This did not at all comfort the Fiscal Feline: He put his tail in his mouth and repeatedly stroked the tassel while swaying back and forth on his legs. And in his nervousness he bit the tail and shrieked in pain.

The very next moment Dakota felt his back tighten and his skin loosen, which was not so much of a reason to be alarmed, except that just when he thought there were no more out-of-the-way things that could happen, his spine began to curve forward and his skin started to have folds. He put his hand up to his face—the nails at the tips of his fingers had become somewhat brittle—and found cracks in the skin. Soon he bore enough wrinkles to resemble an old catcher's mitt and said in a trembling voice, "Holy seeds, whatever happened to my skin?"

Shocked and confused, Dakota scratched his head, but just as he did so, white hair fell to his shoulders, and he gaped. He felt around his scalp for a moment or two, searching for his precious Elvis-like hair, but only met strands on the sides of his head. "Holy seeds! My hair has fallen out!" he cried in a shrill and passionate voice.

At first poor Dakota thought the last medicine he had taken—Sveltezac—and the last thing he had eaten—chips—or all that drinking at the bar—oh, he knew he would live to regret it—were starting to have their effects on him, and it worried him a great deal because the effects were signs of aging, which of course had no cure. "Holy seeds, I must have aged twenty years!"

And old Dakota figured that it would be best to not take any more medicine, unless he absolutely had to, for they seemed to do funny things to him that he couldn't imagine.

But on second thought, there might be a miracle drug or food that could reverse the effects because in the New World nothing was impossible.

"Where is Dr. Quack when you need him?" Dakota lamented to himself.

"I don't see how I could help you, as I am multitasking," the Cuckoo Bird said; she was busy recording the minutes—she was actually doing this and not doodling—while randomly punching the keyboard.

"I don't need your help," Dakota said.

"You must need something if you are bending over like that."

"I'm sorry," Dakota began in a weak voice, "it's just that my back has grown a hunch."

After a moment or two, the Cuckoo Bird asked rather impatiently, "What do you need?"

"Nothing," Dakota replied, frustrated. "I've aged, that's all."

"Why don't you go age somewhere else?" the Cuckoo Bird said, annoyed.

"Hush! You're aging, also."

"Yes, but I age at a normal pace, not all of a sudden." And she at once flew up to a cuckoo clock—which had a still pendulum so that it did not work—that hung on a wall at the edge of the terrace with her "papers," or sheets of wood, and feather pen as fast as she could go, so as to not waste time, and went inside the clock and slammed the door.

While Dakota and the Cuckoo Bird had gotten into an argument, the Big Boss kept his eyes on the Fiscal Feline and, as the Bird had flown away, called, "Send in the Gorilla!" over the banana phone to the Greenback Squirrel, who used his banana to relay the message just as before.

"Give me one good reason," the Chairman said sharply to the lion, "or we'll fire you this instant, whether you're ashamed or not."

"I have a family—a lioness and a few cubs at the den," the Fiscal Feline began in a trembling voice. "And I have started to make improvements to the meetings, and it is with great pride that I can say that I came up with the idea entirely myself, and—"

"What kind of developments have you made?" the Chairman asked pointedly.

"For starters, the food," the Fiscal Feline replied.

"Of course ordering food from anywhere but the jungle is an improvement," the Chairman said in an offended tone. "What kind of fool do you take me for? Continue!"

"I have a family," the Fiscal Feline went on, "and I want to take the leftover food to the den, so we do not waste it, except the Gorilla—"

Here old Dakota shook his head, disgusted and shocked that the Fiscal Feline of all animals was taking credit for *his* idea. "How unfair!" he thought, and he felt like getting up and telling the Chairman the truth but checked himself, as he did not want to interrupt the performance review—that would be rude.

"—the Gorilla keeps taking and wasting all the food. Completely out of control!" the Fiscal Feline finished.

Just then the 800-pound Gorilla barged into the space, beat his chest, and roared, "I do not!"

"Yes, you do," the Fiscal Feline argued. "You hog everything, and no one can stop you, not even me, the lion who should be the King of the Jungle." Then he muttered, "If only I had more courage."

"No, I don't! And even if I did, I can't help it. I'm 800 pounds!" the Gorilla shot back.

"Leave weight out of this," the Chairman said sharply. "We don't want any lawsuits."

Sameer Garach

"Well, ask the Cuckoo Bird, she can attest . . ." the Fiscal Feline trailed off, looking anxiously at the Bird's cubicle to see if he could call her over, but she was nowhere to be found.

"There are other improvements that can be made," the Fiscal Feline began afresh, "such as getting a new cuckoo clock from a black forest. And we've already made progress. For example, the meeting before last we took too long, as the Cuckoo Bird recorded the hours. And the last meeting was too short, as she recorded the seconds. Now she's recording the minutes, and we're finally on schedule."

"Well, that's good. But where did the Cuckoo Bird go?" the Chairman questioned. "Did she ever return from happy hour?"

"That I can't say," the Fiscal Feline replied.

"You must know where your team is," the Chairman said in a severe tone, "or we'll never know how to manage the food properly, and you'll be fired!"

At this the wretched Fiscal Feline dropped his tail, got down on his knees, and started to beg with praying hands, "My *pride*, dear bosses—"

"Swallow your *pride*!" the Chairman screamed with passion.

In another moment the Fiscal Feline gasped in shock, then looked puzzled, and Dakota chuckled at the workplace miscommunication and thought, "I think he means his family. Sometimes you say one thing, but mean another." He smiled to himself, having remembered what he'd learned from Milky.

Then the Fiscal Feline tried again with, "I have a family, dear bosses."

And Dakota looked around with his head held high, very proud of himself for guessing what the cat meant.

"That's the best you can come up with?" the Chairman said sharply. "Keep your job and get out of my sight!"

In the next moment the Fiscal Feline hurried out the boardroom with, of course, his tail between his legs.

"Just reach out to the corporate gestapo—the HR Drones; they'll remove whoever we fire quietly," the Big Boss shouted to the Greenback Squirrel over the banana. But the Fiscal Feline had taken the banana off the Squirrel's desk before the rodent could make the call.

"Put it on speaker," the Chairman said to the Big Boss, and the Big Boss put the banana down and pressed it. "Call in the barista!" the Chairman yelled.

The Greenback Squirrel swallowed and sweated, unable to find the banana, then hurried into the boardroom and said in a trembling voice, "Sir, sirs, the phone is missing. It may be the monkeys again."

The Chairman sighed. "Ugh, them and their monkey business." Then he screamed, "Moose!" When the large deer turned around on his stump to face his caller, the Chairman added rather loudly, "Can you come here for a second?"

"Oh yah, can you give me a minute?" the Moose replied in his peculiar accent.

The Chairman smacked his lips and shouted, "Yeah." Then he faced the Big Boss and said in a subdued tone, "He'll be . . . here in a minute."

The Big Boss and Chairman stared at each other for a moment or two as they waited for the Moose's arrival. Seeing that the employee would take longer than expected, the Chairman felt the table and knocked on it out of boredom and said at last, "What is this log table made of—hickory?"

The Big Boss observed the table, then answered in a meek voice, "I think it's cypress."

"Cypress is nice."

"Yeah . . . cypress is good," the Big Boss remarked just as the Moose came in, and with a cup of coffee, which made the other two in the room bite their lips and take big whiffs, especially when the large deer drank some before their very eyes.

"Tell us why we shouldn't fire you," the Chairman demanded at once.

Suddenly, the Moose spit out coffee beans and spilled them on his apron, very surprised by the question, and exclaimed, "Aw geez!" After some seconds he replied, "Dontchaknow, the office runs on coffee."

The Chairman, for assurances, looked at the Big Boss, who said in a measured tone, "That's not a good enough response."

"Well, I didn't want it to come to this, as I do like coffee," the Chairman began with an air of melancholy. Then he continued rather sternly, "We have no choice but to fire you if you cannot come up with a better response."

"Uff da!" the Moose exclaimed. He hesitated before answering, and Dakota worried that he would be fired (for, you see, the Moose didn't know how to make coffee). "Good ideas come from brainstorming. Do you agree?"

"Why, yes," the Chairman replied.

"And to come up with great ideas, you need synergy. Am I right?"

"I couldn't agree more."

"But you can't spell *synergy* without *energy*."

The Chairman blinked a few times, then said, "I suppose you can't."

"Now, energy comes from coffee. So, good ideas begin with brainstorming, and great ideas begin with coffee," the Moose finished.

The Chairman turned to the Big Boss, who remarked, "That's a good answer," which was quickly followed up by the Chairman, whose brown nose glowed as he said, "Yes, a very fine response."

Dakota smiled; the large deer passed the test.

"Oh yah." Here the Moose tipped his cup toward them and remarked rather wisely, "How do you think I came up with it?"

This made for a quick laugh from the Chairman, who stopped at once when it occurred to him that the Big Boss was not sharing in the good times and, back to business, asked, "What is your coffee made of?"

"Best-in-class coffee beans, from Minnesota, mostly," the Moose replied. "And so are the coffee cakes."

"And why is that?" the Chairman asked.

"Because the company does not have any money," the Cuckoo Bird interrupted, having flown in just as the question had been put to the Moose.

"Cage that Cuckoo Bird!" the Big Boss yelled, and the golden fox on top of his head shrieked a scream-y howl. "Fire her! Get her out! Pluck her feathers! Off with the minutes like that!"

Here the whole terrace office became confused, and for quite some time, getting the Cuckoo Bird back to her cubicle, and when they finally did, the minutes she was supposed to be recording had to be recovered, which some workers believed would take overtime to accomplish.

"My goodness. That bird made me nearly fall off my chair!" the Chairman remarked, and Dakota did not think this was possible, as the chair was glued to his behind. "There's no need to worry," the Chairman announced to the company. "Our finances are in order," which was a great relief to the workers, who were already on edge because of the performance review. In another moment the Chairman returned to the Moose and said, "Continue with what you were saying."

"The coffee is raw, not processed," the Moose explained.

"So, it's all natural?"

"You betcha," the Moose replied. "Processed foods are bad, dontchaknow."

"Yes, I've read about that," the Chairman said. "Very well, run along and get back to work." The Moose left just as he had come, coffee cup in hand, and once he was gone, the Chairman leaned over to the Big Boss and said, "My superior, I think it is your turn to handle the reviews. I need a break."

Dakota watched the Big Boss go down a paper in front of him on the table, eager to know who would be the next employee to be yanked-and-ranked. "They haven't fired anyone yet," he said to himself, then with great delight, "At that rate I don't think they ever will."

Just then the Big Boss called out, "The new guy."

Here Dakota looked about the terrace office and wondered whom it was. Suddenly, he felt a tap on his shoulder and found nearby the Greenback Squirrel. In another moment the little rodent stirred great surprise in him when he said, "That's you, Dakota!"

Chapter 13: Dakota's Refusal

"Me?" old Dakota cried (for, you see, it had been so long since he had been hired that it never occurred to him that he might lose his job one day). He had quite forgotten that he had aged in appearance and body in the last half hour, so when he got up and started about, he tumbled to the grass in his haste, disturbing all the workers from their business, and there he lay sprawling in pain. Suddenly, a terrible image of that one disturbing time when he fell off his bicycle and couldn't get up flashed through his mind.

"We are very sorry," one said after another in a tone of great worry that sounded like they were acting.

And Dakota wondered, "Why are they apologizing if they didn't do anything wrong?" In the next minute or two, they started to grab his arms and help him regain his footing while he shrieked out in agony, like he had done when people tried to pick him up after the bicycle accident. In another moment he had a feeling that all would be okay and he might have overreacted, then yelled, "Stuff your pretend-sorries in a sack, fakers!"

"It is a great tragedy that this has happened in our workplace. Send the new guy my apologies," the Chairman added—facing the Greenback Squirrel—to the growing snowball of fake apologies. "Legal will take it from here," he said, looking hard at poor old Dakota as though he were ready to fight the hobbled man to his death.

It occurred to Dakota once he was up that he couldn't stand without tipping over, for his back had curved that much, so he requested someone help him to the boardroom. In another minute Jenny brought him a small branch—which the Gorilla had broken off from a tree—to use as a cane, and Dakota suddenly remembered a riddle he had heard at school and said to himself, "Why, it must be the evening, for now I have three legs!"

As soon as the distraction started to come to an end and the workers had finished expressing their sympathies, they returned to being very busy, punching the keyboards and doodling on papers without any principle of organization, all except the 800-pound Gorilla, who knew that no one could get him to do anything he had no desire to, as he was so big and powerful.

"What do you make of the *role*?" the Chairman asked Dakota once he entered the boardroom.

"I did not at all like the *roll*," Dakota said, thinking of his painful tumble.

"Well, finding the right fit is difficult," the Chairman began in a reasonable sort of way, "but there must be something likeable about it?"

"It was awful," Dakota said with a face of worry.

"Hmm, I suppose that is expected, the workload being very heavy," the Chairman said. He turned to the Big Boss, who only shook his head in disagreement and remarked, "Rather unexpected."

"Uh, yes, that is unexpected," the Chairman quickly recovered, and his brown nose glowed. Suddenly, he began to repeatedly kiss the Big Boss on the side of his giant orange head, starting from the lower jaw and working his way up to the temple, which only prompted Dakota to think, "What a kiss-up!" The Chairman continued in a sharp tone, "You should be used to this kind of workload by now, seeing that you are very—" He observed the wrinkles on Dakota's face, his bald head, and his hunchback. "How shall I put this—experienced."

Old, three-legged Dakota yawned, disinterested in hearing that the *roll* should be likeable. In another moment an insect came buzzing down the stone pathway of the terrace, and Dakota could see it was the Drone—now wearing a black leather trench coat—who had been called for earlier. "Hopefully," he thought, "he'll have some fun riddles like the last time we met."

Once the Drone entered the boardroom, came under the large pergola, the Chairman, who had been waiting for the buzzing to stop, yelled, "What on earth took you so long?"

134

To which the Drone explained, in his peculiar accent, "Dude, I'm like totally sorry I couldn't have been here sooner; I was hecka busy doing nothing, like as busy as a bee!"

This cooled the Chairman, who nodded and said, "Excuse my language. Thank you for being a busy bee. It is much appreciated." Of course the Drone nodded in kind, and the whole exchange made Dakota want to laugh. Then the Chairman returned to the matter at hand and said, "According to company policy, anybody over the hill must be fired."

Everybody on the terrace looked at Dakota; but in another moment the animals outside the boardroom went back to work for fear that they might not look busy.

"I'm ten years old," Dakota argued.

"How do you expect me to believe that?" the Chairman asked pointedly.

"When you look old enough to be my grandpa," the Big Boss added.

"Well, I'm not leaving," Dakota said in a decided tone. "It's unfair and a poor reason to get rid of me."

"But you can't do the work anymore," the Chairman said.

"I can fake type and doodle," Dakota fought back.

The Chairman turned pale and addressed the Drone with a low voice. "You heard his argument. What do you think? Can we keep him on board?"

"Dude, maybe it would be good to verify his age from like the employment application," the Drone replied.

To which the Greenback Squirrel interrupted, "I'll get it," and hurried off.

"I don't think he could have been hired if he was like ten," the Drone continued. "But if he did, that would be like epic."

After a minute or two, the Greenback Squirrel returned with the employment application in hand, and the Big Boss inquired, "What does it say?"

"Hold on, hold on, I've just come back," the Greenback Squirrel replied, putting on his glasses and sifting through the pages of the application, as the Drone hovered over him. "Ayuh, it says he was born ten years ago."

"It cannot be!" the Chairman cried, then in a conservative tone to the Big Boss, "Unless HR overlooked this detail in the hiring process, which is possible, you know."

"What does the copy of his driver's license say?" the Big Boss asked.

The Greenback Squirrel went through the pages while the Drone looked on, sweating. "There is no copy of the driver's license. In fact, there is no copy of anything, not a social security card, not a birth certificate, nothing!"

"Perhaps it's been like, misplaced," the Drone suggested.

"What is the handwriting like?" the Chairman asked. "An adult's, I presume."

"No, not at all," the Greenback Squirrel said, "which makes this all the more confusing." Those present exchanged puzzled glances, and the rodent went on. "The handwriting is somewhat lacking in flow—the letters are formed somewhat haltingly—and the script is uneven, and the lines are straight and vertical, not hurried and slanted like an adult's."

"He must have forged the writing!" the Chairman charged. "You know, to make it look like that of a child." The attendees sighed, relieved they had a proper explanation.

"But it is my handwriting," old Dakota pleaded, "and I can prove it." In another moment he took the pen on the table and the application from the Squirrel and proceeded to demonstrate his writing while everyone crowded around him to watch. Once Dakota finished, the group slowly leaned away with puzzled faces, because the writing looked just as it did on the rest of the application. Then Dakota signed his name, hoping they'd be impressed by his John Hancock, and asked, "Do you like my signature?"

They all looked at each other rather confused. The Chairman viewed the last page of the application and noted, "There is no signature," which baffled everyone even more. The Chairman turned to Dakota and said, "If you did fill out this application but did not sign it, then that only makes matters worse. We have nothing to compare your signature to, which gives us more reason to believe there is some mischief at play." And this received applause, as it was one of the few bright things the Chairman had said.

Sameer Garach

"Well, that proves everything," the Big Boss said in a decided tone. "The old man has covered up his age somehow. Get the cannon ready."

"That doesn't prove anything!" Dakota argued, wise enough and brave enough to not be pushed out the door. "Why, you have nothing that says I'm not in fact ten."

"I have your appearance, your hunchback and wrinkles, your bald head," the Big Boss said, then to the Drone, "What do you make of this?"

The Drone at once replied, "We don't employ children; that's illegal. So his appearance is like, all we need, dude; it's totally like, the most important information."

"That is because of the syrup and pills, and—and the junk food I've eaten, the drinks I've had," Dakota cried. "It's all come back to haunt me!"

"Drug use?" the Big Boss said quite pointedly. "That's grounds for firing!"

"Med-i-cine," poor old Dakota pronounced his words slowly so the Big Boss would understand. "I'm not as old as you claim I am, and I can do the work, and—and your evidence is without basis. Stuff your cannon with someone else. You want to fire me only because I seem too old for the job."

"Easy now," the Chairman said in a trembling voice to Dakota, then turning to the Big Boss and swallowing nervously, "We don't want another legal problem. He's already got that tumble against us."

The Big Boss stared at the table for a moment or two and appeared to be processing the situation they suddenly found themselves in. "There seems to be a misunderstanding," he said in a calming tone to Dakota. "I hear your side of things. Now your application, let's talk that, see how all this happened."

"Here you go," the Greenback Squirrel said as he handed the employment application to the Big Boss, who passed it off to his colleague.

The Chairman examined a few pages, then came to a stop and narrowed his eyes on one. "It says here your highest education is fourth grade. Is this true?"

"Yes, of course it is. I cannot lie and say I'm in a higher grade. That would be dishonest," old, three-legged Dakota answered with great pride, glad to get an opportunity to show off his character.

At this the Chairman blinked several times, and his face wore a frown. "He tells the truth, yet his appearance tells a lie!" he said quite shocked, then in a tone of melancholy to himself, "I'm satisfied and perplexed at the same time."

"Pick out another question," the Big Boss ordered, staring hard at Dakota and turning red in the face. "He didn't take the application seriously—a total disregard for the system!"

And all the others, except Dakota, nodded in agreement and said similar things of the following sort: "That sounds right."

The Chairman flipped through the pages once more, then began reading aloud the questions and answers, his face hidden from view, as he held the papers up high. "Address: 'I live on a hill'—phone number: 'I don't remember, but I can ask my mom'—where do you see yourself in five years: 'ninth grade and on the baseball team'—skills: 'dribbling a basketball with either hand, can throw a perfect spiral, spelling words'—hobbies: 'playing with my dog Bernie, recess, playing with my teddy bear.'" The Chairman tossed the application onto the table in front of him and frowned at Dakota. "Is this all a big joke to you?"

"If anyone can find a good laugh in there," Dakota said, his wisdom and courage kicking in, "I'll be the first to ask, 'What's so funny?' I should think there's no joke in it."

Here the Greenback Squirrel muttered, with sympathy in his voice, "You guys, he says he's serious about it," but none of the others attempted to take pity on poor old Dakota.

"If this application has been filled out with the seriousness and respect it's due," the Chairman said, "that saves us a world of problems, because then it is clear that you shouldn't have been hired in the first place. And yet I don't know how you did!" He viewed the application near his face again and continued. "Nor do I know how you managed to get so high up on the Ladder of Diminishing Rungs—this has all the telltale signs of a corporate scandal! Don't you have any *principles*?"

"I have one *principal*," Dakota said, thinking of his school's leader.

The Chairman stared at the old man for a moment, then raised his brows, expecting, but Dakota only mirrored his facial expression. After not receiving an explanation, the Chairman continued. "Anyway, I see some seriousness in these responses; after all, it says you can spell words, which is something we need, considering all the typos in emails we have"—he put the papers down and looked at Dakota—"though I would have put it more professionally, don't you think?"

Old Dakota shook his head and said, rather confused, "I would?" He most certainly wouldn't because he didn't know how else he should have written his response, except for making it in cursive.

"Yes, like 'skills in communication,' or some such. But still," the Chairman said, and he continued with the answers but in a disappointed sort of way to himself, "'I live on a hill'—you could have been more precise—'ninth grade and the baseball team'—I don't get this at all—'can throw a perfect spiral'—what use does that have in the workplace?—'playing with my teddy bear'—sounds like you have a strange infatuation with stuffed animals—"

"But see, there's no joke," Dakota interrupted. "It's all very serious."

"Ugh . . . yeah," the Chairman said rather doubtfully. "This does not sound like it was a serious attempt to answer the questions." Then he turned to the Big Boss. "Shall I go on?"

"No!" the Big Boss shouted angrily, and suddenly, the golden fox on top of his head stood, alert. In another moment the Big Boss threw the pen at the Drone and yelled, "How did you miss all of this?"

At this the Drone sulked and moved into a corner of the pergola, where he muttered, "Dude, that stings!"

"These are not the answers of a child," the Chairman announced boldly. "They are the answers of a man who's turned so old he's senile!" The room turned quiet as they all pondered this, then looked at Dakota with defeated half-smiles. "This is an issue for HR. Let the Drone look into the matter."

"No!" the Big Boss scoffed. "Fire him first—then determine why he should be."

"All applesauce!" Dakota shouted. "Firing without having a reason!"

"Simmer down, new guy!" the Big Boss screamed, red as a tomato and about to burst.

"Never!" Dakota shot back.

"Pie him in the face! And stuff him in the cannon!" the Big Boss yelled at the top of his lungs, and the fox let out a scream-y howl. The Drone closed in on Dakota while the Squirrel summoned the 800-pound Gorilla just in case Dakota proved more difficult than originally thought.

"I'm not going anywhere!" Dakota said to the Big Boss; he was now wise enough to see through the game that had been played on him from the start to get his old, three-legged self out the door. "You're nothing but a bully!"

"We have to fire somebody." The Chairman stuck his glowing brown nose in the air. "Unfortunately, it is you!"

"That's it," Dakota snapped, his face marked with fury. "You keep pushing me and pushing me! Now I've got no choice but to tell you who you should fire—the Drone!"

"Dude! That is not cool," the Drone said at once in an offended tone. "I get that you're butthurt because you got fired, but there's no need to take it out on me. If I wasn't here, the company would like, fail."

But Dakota continued angrier than before. "My butt doesn't hurt! You don't know what you're doing. You hire the wrong people and try to cover your mistakes, and an organization is only as good as its people." He smiled to himself for coming up with a lesson, and the room became silent.

"Fire him!" the Big Boss suddenly shouted and pointed to poor old Dakota.

Just then the 800-pound Gorilla took the farewell cake and threw it at Dakota, who luckily ducked at the right moment so that the cake hit the Big Boss in the face. While everyone stared and gasped in shock, Dakota chanced upon a little opening in the clamor and made a run for it. They all chased him with the Drone leading the pack, and Dakota screamed, full of fear.

Of course they caught up with him—he had the body of an old man—then dragged him to the cannon while he repeatedly shouted, "No!" Despite his efforts, they stuffed him in the cannon, lit the fuse, and fired him.

In the next moment his heart jumped, his eyes burst open, and he tried to get up, except he found himself sitting on a bench under the shade of a tree next to his mother, Columbia, who at once warned him not to move, as a pair of bees hovered near them.

"How was your nap?" she asked.

"I had a dream!" Dakota said, watching the bees buzz away. He told her everything he could remember, and when he finished, his mother rubbed his head in a playful manner and said, "You've got quite an imagination. Come on, it's time to go home." So Dakota gathered his baseball and glove and returned to one side of the car's back seat, then watched downtown pass by in the window all the while thinking how amazing his dream had been.

While Columbia drove the car in the setting sun, she couldn't help but think about little Dakota and his dream, until she forgot about the traffic and signals and started making the stops and turns automatically, and she began daydreaming as follows:

First, she imagined little Dakota as he was. Once again, the boy sat staring out the window, his baseball cap turned a bit to the side, his eyes starting to shut, as he gradually drifted into another slumber—the mother could hear the whistling of her son's breathing slow, and see that funny sniffle of his little nose to keep it from running—and still as the mother listened, or attempted to with the noise that comes from driving in the city, the whole dream world enveloped her and all the animals came to life.

The Greenback Squirrel hurried down hopscotch lane—the buzzing Drone posed many a question—the Black Rat came out of the sewer and splashed in the pool of money—she could see the wasted food as the 800-pound Gorilla and his colleagues had called a useless meeting—and hear the Big Boss threatening his employees with firings—the image of the goldfish-cracker sucking on the coffee beans flashed before her, while the roasted seeds spilled around its tank to keep up the atmosphere—she pictured the doodling of the White Mouse—the moo of Milky, the punching of the keyboards, and the calls for the Drone echoed in the air and meshed with the arrogant boasting of the piteous Plush Bear.

Columbia drove on, paying little attention to how far she'd traveled and how much was still left to go, and envisioned the curious dream, though she knew that all she had to do was wake up, and all would turn to the sights and sounds of the park—the hopscotch game would only be chalk on the pathway, and the pool of money, coins in the fountain—the wasted food would turn out to be overstuffed garbage cans, and the Big Boss's shouting to a boy who cried fire in jest—and the typing, the coffee beans, and all the other happenings, would reveal themselves to be the confused clamor of her personal office, as she had brought her work and coffee to the park—while the boasts of some child in the distance would take the place of the Plush Bear's arrogant claims.

Dakota and the American Dream

As the car pulled up to their home's driveway, she imagined how her son would one day chase his own American Dream; and how he would not grow old but remain a child at heart; and how he might gather around his coworkers for happy hour, and make their faces glow with interesting work experiences; and how he would reflect on his journey, and find a pleasure in the joys and sorrows of this Land of Opportunity, remembering his own dreams as a child, and wondering whether he achieved his American Dream.

The End

CONNECT WITH THE AUTHOR

I hope you enjoyed *Dakota and the American Dream* as much as I enjoyed writing it. I invite you to connect with me at any of the following coordinates. I look forward to hearing from you!

Website: http://www.sameergarach.com
Facebook: http://www.facebook.com/sameergarach
Pinterest: http://www.pinterest.com/sameergarach
Instagram: http://www.instagram.com/sameergarach
Spotify: http://open.spotify.com/user/sameergarach
LinkedIn: http://www.linkedin.com/in/sameergarach
Goodreads: http://www.goodreads.com/sameergarach

DISCUSSION GUIDE

1. What do you like best/least about this book?
2. What book or movies does this remind you of?
3. Which characters did you like the best/least?
4. Match the following characters to the appropriate American regional dialect.

HR Drone	Alabama/Southern
Black Rat	Spanglish
Greenback Squirrel	Texas/Southern
Josefina the Skunk	New York
Mermaid	Boston
Moose	Fargo/North Dakota/ Minnesota
Milky	African-American Vernacular English
Jenny	California

5. Whom would you cast if you were making a movie about this book?
6. What do you think of the book's title? How does it relate to the book's contents? What other title would you select?
7. Would you read another book by this author? Why or why not?

www.ingramcontent.com/pod-product-compliance
Lightning Source LLC
Chambersburg PA
CBHW022020170626
46808CB00003B/997